The Ysabel Kid and Waco had turned their horses and were galloping back. Seeing that he had caught the others' attention, the Kid pointed toward their left. Swinging their gaze in the required direction, the women, Dusty, and O'Day received a shock. Some twenty or more *Kweharehnuh* warriors sat their horses on a ridge slightly over a quarter of a mile away.

"Whee doggie!" Dusty breathed, and hefted his Winchester carbine so that the Indians could see it. "Show them your rifle, mister."

"Shoot?" O'Day inquired as he did as Dusty had said.

"Just show them we've got repeaters, first off," Dusty corrected him.

"Now what?" Emma demanded with surprising calm.

" 'Less we're lucky," Dusty answered, "some of us are about to get killed."

Go Back to Hell

J. T. EDSON

A DELL BOOK

Published by
Dell Publishing
a division of
Bantam Doubleday Dell Publishing Group, Inc.
666 Fifth Avenue
New York, New York 10103

ISBN: 0-440-21033-X

Printed in the United States of America

Published simultaneously in Canada

February 1992

10 9 8 7 6 5 4 3 2 1

OPM

Go Back to Hell

1
YOU'RE ALL HONEST MEN

"There's a bank down to Corsicana we could take," Dick Shalupka remarked, lounging at ease by the fire. "Ain't but an itty-bitty one-hoss town. We could go in and wouldn't have no trouble in coming out rich."

"You're talking wild, Dick," protested Bernie Stoll. "There ain't but the three of us left."

"So what'd you have us do, Bernie?" demanded Henny Shalupka, indignant at the implied criticism of his elder brother. "Go back to working cattle at thirty a month?"

None of the trio had ever worked cattle, even at less than thirty dollars a month, or performed any other task that was demanding in terms of effort and sweat. Until adopting what had struck them as the easier and more genteel occupation of outlaw, they had worked—when driven by dire necessity and for as short a period as possible—at various menial tasks around the Kansas trail-end towns.

However, even if it only deluded themselves, the pretense

of having once been cowhands implied a higher social standing than any one of them had attained.

The fire's light threw an eerie red glow across a clearing
among a grove of post oaks on the banks of Lake Kemp in
Baylor County, Texas. It illuminated a camp set up in a slov-
enly, haphazard manner for a night under the bright stars
and quarter moon. Four horses, hobbled by the forelegs,
grazed restlessly on the edge of the lake. Around the fire lay
a quartet of saddles. Standing on their skirts, three of them
would have told any West-wise observer that their owners
were not connected with the cattle industry. No cowhand
would ever risk causing damage to his most important item
of equipment by setting it down in such a manner. A bedroll
was spread by each saddle and a rifle rested on every seat.

There was an almost family likeness about the three young
men, although Stoll was not related to the Shalupkas. All
were tall and lean, their faces hinting at sly, dissipated na-
tures. They wore clothes of the style favored by trail hands
who had been paid off at the end of a cattle drive, just a
shade too loud and ornate for everyday usage. The garments
were dirty and showed traces of voluntary neglect. White-
handled Colt 1860 Army revolvers hung, in what were sold
to the unwary or inexperienced as fast-draw holsters, at their
sides.

"Ain't no call for talk like that, Henny," Dick grunted.
"Hell, Bernie-boy, we know how to take a bank, or a stagecoach. Damn it, we've rid with Joey Pinter long enough to
handle things without him."

"A three-way split licks sharing 'tween four or five any ole
day," Henny chortled.

"Hold your voice down!" Dick ordered, darting a pointed
glance to the southern edge of the clearing.

"Who cares if he hears us?" Henny asked; but apparently
he did, for he had pitched his tones to a much lower level. "I
ain't sure's I wants him to go on bossing the gang."

"You reckon we can take that old bank in Corsicana?"
Stoll inquired, wishing to avoid being brought into a discussion on the leadership of their gang.

"It'll be easier'n falling off a log," Dick promised. "All we have to do is go in—"

"Good evening, gentlemen."

The voice, polite in its inflection, came from the shadows beyond the northern fringe of the firelight. At the first word, the trio let out mutually startled gasps and tried to rise hurriedly with hands grabbing toward the butts of guns. They stared at the shape, looming up darker than the surrounding blackness, that came toward them.

Holding out his hands at shoulder height to show his empty palms, a tall man approached the fire. All in all, he made a somewhat unusual and almost theatrical figure to be emerging out of a Texas post-oak grove. A black stovepipe hat tilted at a jaunty angle on a thatch of long, flaming-red hair. With almost V-shaped rufous brows over deep-set eyes, a hook nose, and tight lips above a sharp chin, he had a Mephistophelian cast of features. A black opera cloak with a red satin lining was draped over his shoulders. He wore a black broadcloth coat and matching vest. His dress shirt had one of those newfangled celluloid collars, with a black silk cravat knotted bow-tie fashion, and wide, hard-starched detachable cuffs. More suited to Western traveling conditions, his yellowish-brown nankeen trousers were tucked into low-heeled black Wellington-leg boots. Looking out of place against his other attire, a wide brown leather gun belt, with a large, ornate brass buckle, slanted down to his right thigh. In a contoured holster reposed an ivory-handled Colt Cavalry Model Peacemaker.

"I hope that my coming up just now did not startle you," the newcomer said, in a friendly voice that belied his sardonic expression.

"Wha—who—?" Dick spluttered, first of his party to regain even a semblance of speech.

"I saw your fire and came over to ask if I might share it for the night," the man announced calmly.

"Huh?" croaked Dick, too surprised by the stranger's arrival to make any more useful contribution to the conversation.

"I've never been much for bedding down alone," the man continued, coming to a halt alongside the unoccupied bedroll and looking across the fire at the trio. "Maybe I'd best introduce myself. The name's O'Day. My friends call me 'Break.'"

Lowering his hands to his sides, but keeping them outside the cloak, the newcomer had the attitude of one who had cracked a joke and was waiting for a response to it.

"'Break'?" Dick repeated, while his companions looked equally uncomprehending. Then he cut loose with a guffaw of understanding. "Break O'Day. Hey! Do you fellers cotton on to it?"

"Oh, sure," Henny agreed, and squatted on his heels.

Clearly sharing the younger brother's opinion that the newcomer was harmless, Dick and Stoll also settled down on their bedrolls.

"Help yourself to the coffee, happen you're so minded," Dick offered, indicating the pot that bubbled and steamed on the edge of the fire. "We don't have any food."

"The coffee'll be all I need," the man assured him, but made no move to help himself. "And I've always found that it helps to know who I'm addressing."

Coldly avaricious eyes studied the man, taking note of his expensive clothing, the gold cuff links and well-tooled gun belt. That was one of the new, metallic cartridge Colt revolvers and looked to be of the Best Citizen's blued finish. Undoubtedly he would have money on him, while his horse, saddle, and rigging—wherever they might be—would offer even more loot. To three young outlaws in serious financial straits, he had the appearance of manna from heaven.

If the man felt any anxiety over the trio's scrutiny, he gave no sign of it. Standing by the fire, he might have been safe in the bar of an exclusive dude sporting club for all the concern he showed. In fact, he displayed an air of calm superiority as if satisfied that he had inadvertently blundered into the society of his social inferiors.

"I'm Tom Smith and this's my brother, Bill," Dick introduced, wanting to learn more about their visitor before deciding upon a line of action. "This here's Jack Brown."

"You took a big chance coming up on us like that, mister," Henny went on, annoyed by the man's attitude and wanting to throw a scare into him. "We might've been owlhoots."

"Anybody can see you're all honest men," the stranger protested. "You're not the sort to go robbing stagecoaches, nor even a bank in some one-horse town like Corsicana. Now if you'd been somebody like Joey Pinter—"

None of the trio could have been termed quick-witted, so the inference behind the man's words did not strike them straightaway. Slowly the feeling crept into their skulls that he had just mentioned a subject that they had been discussing before his arrival. Yet he claimed to have come directly through the grove and to the fire. He should not have known about their professional interest in stagecoaches and the bank at Corsicana. There had also been his reference to Joey Pinter. That had hardly been inspired by coincidence, not when he was addressing leading members of the selfsame outlaw's gang. Several unpleasant reasons for his eavesdropping upon what should have been a strictly private conversation sprang—or crawled slowly—into their minds.

For all his outlandish dude clothing, Break O'Day must be a peace officer of some kind. Or, even worse, a bounty hunter who tracked down and killed wanted men for the price on their heads. Neither the Shalupka brothers nor Stoll paused to consider that their activities had failed to bring down such a penalty as having a reward offered for their capture. To their way of thinking, O'Day had located them for his own financial gain.

Well, the trio figured there was a right smart answer to *that*.

"Now there's some'd say you know a heap too much," Dick warned, starting to straighten his knees and lift himself erect.

"A hell of a lot too much!" Dick's brother confirmed, also beginning to rise and grabbing for his holstered Colt.

"I fail to see what you mean, gentlemen," O'Day replied

mildly, resting his elbows lightly against the sides of the
cloak and holding his upturned, open hands toward the
brothers.

Stoll made their meaning even plainer as he came to his
feet with a lurching thrust and joined his companions in
reaching hipward for guns.

"Kill the son of a bitch!" was his contribution.

Through all the signs of consternation and aggression,
O'Day continued to stand like a statue. Although his gun
belt and holster had really been designed to facilitate a rapid
withdrawal of the seven-and-a-half-inch-barreled Colt—not
as a cheaply made imitation for purchase by would-be *pis-
toleros* who knew no better than to entrust their lives to
shoddy workmanship—he seemed to be badly positioned to
make the most of his advantages. The broadcloth coat was
unbuttoned, but it and the cloak would both be in the way as
his right hand tried to reach the Colt's butt. Nor were his
hands held anything like ready for making a draw.

Having observed the extended, empty, upturned palms,
the three young men were confident that they could give
O'Day an unforgettable, permanent lesson in manners. By
the time they were through, that blasted dude would know
better than to sneak up on experienced desperadoes and listen to their private conversations, although it was unlikely
that the lesson would do him any good.

All those thoughts rolled ponderously through the heads
of the Shalupka brothers and Bernie Stoll during the brief
time they were rising with the intention of killing the tall,
menacing, yet empty-handed stranger.

Suddenly, miraculously it seemed to the trio, O'Day's
hands were no longer empty. His elbows made pressing motions against his sides. Almost instantly two stubby Remington Double Deringers flashed from inside his shirt sleeves.
Gripped in the jaws of a slender metal rod, which pushed it
into exactly the right position, each weapon came to a halt
where his fingers could enfold its butt. Without taking even
the split second that would have been required to turn the

weapons from horizontal to vertical, O'Day thumbed back the hammers.

Flame spurted from the muzzle of the right-hand weapon's upper superposed barrel. Its .41-caliber bullet drove a hole into Dick Shalupka's head. An instant later, the lower tube of the left-hand Remington hurled its load into the center of Bernie Stoll's chest. Both of the young men pitched backward with their guns not clear of leather.

Although Henny Shalupka had been granted the opportunity to draw his Colt, the fate of his brother and Stoll caused him to freeze into immobility. That did not save him. Back clicked the two Deringers' hammers, the firing pins automatically rising or moving downward so as to reach the edges of the unfired rimless cartridges when released to carry out their functions. O'Day turned his weapons to vertical. With his face looking even more devilish in the flickering red glow of the fire, he squeezed both triggers. The bullets took Henny in the left breast, ending unsaid the plea he had been about to make for his life.

Even as Henny followed his brother and Stoll to the ground, O'Day detected sounds that implied that he might have further need for weapons. A voice let out a startled yelp and then there was a crashing among the bushes to the south of the clearing as the speaker ran toward it.

Swiftly the man reached a decision. There would be no time to reload the little hideout pistols. Nor, if the person making the noisy approach was who O'Day suspected, did he fancy using such short-ranged weapons. Throwing a disgusted glance at the three shapes that lay jerking spasmodically in death throes, O'Day swung on his heel. That was the worst of the Deringers, ideal as they might be as concealment armaments. A man could not do fancy shooting with them. So O'Day had been compelled to shoot to kill instead of trying to wing one of the trio, keeping him alive and able to answer questions. However, if the sounds from the south meant anything, O'Day would soon have another—and probably better—source of information.

Dropping the left-hand Deringer into his jacket pocket

while striding across the clearing in the direction from which he had come, O'Day used his free palm to shove the other weapon into the shirt's cuff. Pressing it until the catch of the spring-holdout device attached to his forearm held it in place, he drew the Peacemaker. Taking cover behind the trunk of a tree, he raised the long-barreled revolver in both hands and squinted experimentally along the sights.

A stocky young man appeared in the other side of the clearing. He wore the same style of clothing and armament as O'Day's victims. Nor did the newcomer appear to exceed their intellect. Bounding in what should have been an agile manner onto the moss-covered trunk of a fallen tree, he slipped. With a yell of surprise, which turned to pain an instant later, he landed awkwardly. There was a dull crack and his left leg buckled under him. Going down, he lost his hold of the Army Colt he had drawn while running to investigate. Then he tried to reach and pick it up.

"Leave it be, young feller!" O'Day ordered, sighting the revolver without revealing himself. "Then I'll come out and tend your hurts."

Forgetting his desire to be armed, the newcomer clutched at his left leg.

"I don't know who you be, mister," the man groaned. "But I'm hurting bad and need help."

"And I'll give it," O'Day promised, walking forward with the Peacemaker dangling almost negligently in his right fist. "Try to ease 'round and sit with your back to that deadfall."

"Lord!" the injured man moaned as he obeyed. "It hurts!"

"I'd say that's likely," O'Day admitted. "That was a nasty fall you took. Possibly I can do something to ease you though. What do I call you?"

"Dipper Dixon," the man answered.

"Then you just rest as easy as you can, Dipper," O'Day instructed. "I'm going to have to ruin your pants, but it's for your own good."

"Wha-what happened to them?" Dixon inquired, indicating his companions.

"I don't know. Heard shooting as I was coming through

the trees toward the fire. When I arrived, they were all down. Then I heard you coming and thought I'd better stay hidden until I could see who you might be. As soon as I saw your face, I knew I didn't need to worry. Anybody can see that you're a better class of man than those three."

There were several inconsistencies about the story, but Dixon was in no condition to notice them. He had not cared greatly about his companions' fate. The only bond between himself, the Shalupka brothers, and Stoll had died a week ago. It had only been a matter of time before they had separated for good.

Having satisfied the man's curiosity, O'Day took a Russell Barlow knife from his jacket's right pocket and opened its blade. Gently, as if handling something fragile and priceless, he slit the seam of Dixon's trousers' left leg. After examining the injured limb, he collected two of the rifles from by the fire. Cutting strips from a blanket, he used it to hold the rifles as splints after he had drawn the leg back to its normal shape. Dixon fainted before he had finished working.

"You'll be all right in a few weeks," O'Day promised, when the young man had recovered. Fetching him a cup of coffee from the fire, the dude continued, "Now I'm going to help you some more."

"How?" Dixon wanted to know.

"First you have to help me," O'Day countered.

"If I can," Dixon said warily.

"Tell me where I can find Joey Pinter."

"Who'd he—"

"Friend, *friend*," O'Day interrupted chidingly. "Do you know why I'm taking all this time and trouble to help you?"

"Nope," the young outlaw admitted.

"Because I believe that you're worth saving and giving a second chance. You're not like those three. They were bad all through, but you're not."

"Who-who are you, mister?"

"My name's O'Day. I'm Governor Stanton Howard's Chief Amnesty Inspector."

"What's that?"

"You'll probably know that the governor has promised to end the current wave of lawlessness in the sovereign state of Texas?" O'Day asked.

"I've heard tell of it," Dixon agreed bitterly.

Most outlaws in the Lone Star State grew bitter, or profane, when speaking of Governor Stanton Howard's vigorous policies regarding themselves. Unlike the Davis Reconstruction Administration, the present head of Texas's political affairs was pressing hard to contain the outlaw element's activities. Brought back to replace the corrupt, inefficient state police, the Texas Rangers were running the various criminal bands ragged and generally making life unbearable for any man with a price on his head.

"The governor is a humane man," O'Day went on. "He knows that a whole lot of young fellers were pushed into a life of crime through no fault of their own. He doesn't want them hounded down like the real bad *hombres*. So he's offering an amnesty and free pardon to those young men."

"What's that mean?"

"The men he's after won't be outlaws anymore. That's why I'm out here. It's my duty to find such men, interview them, and decide on whether they are deserving of the amnesty."

"And you're figuring on Joey Pinter as one of 'em?"

Dixon might lack intelligence, but he was smart enough to know that the brutal, murderous Joey Pinter would be an unlikely candidate for a pardon. Not even the most humane man in the world would risk his political career by publicly forgiving Joey Pinter's many crimes.

"Is that likely?" O'Day scoffed, reading the other's thoughts. "But I know that you rode with him." He waved a hand to silence Dixon's protest before it could be uttered. "Don't try to shield him, which's what you planned to do. I've read your character and you're not a liar. If I thought you was, I'd not offer to help you."

"*You're* going to help *me*?" Dixon yelped.

"I am. But I must know where Pinter is, then I can arrange

things so that he doesn't come and interfere with you in your new life."

"He won't do that. He was killed by Ed Caxton up in Hell."

"In . . . ?" queried O'Day.

"Hell," Dixon repeated. "It's a town in the Palo Duro country."

"I thought that the Indians still controlled that region," O'Day remarked.

"They sure do. Hell's smack-dab in the middle of the *Kwe-harehnuh* Comanches' home range."

"And the Indians don't molest you?"

"Neither going there, nor coming back." Dixon grinned. "The mayor sees to that. Right smart feller he is for a dude. He's got them Antelopes eating out of his hand, thinking he's a mighty strong medicine man. What I heard, he does the damnedest thing to keep them that way. They say he saws his wife in half."

"I've heard tell of it being done," O'Day admitted, but there was a glow of interest in his eyes that did not match his casual tone. "Did you see the mayor do it?"

"Nope," Dixon replied, regretfully. "Way I heard it, though, it's a sight to see. He's got this cute li'l brown-haired woman all dressed in just about the shortest Injun gal's frock you ever did see—"

"You say that Pinter was killed there," O'Day interrupted. "By the law?"

"Naw. There's no law in Hell, 'cepting the mayor. It was Ed Caxton who made wolf bait of Joey. Him's robbed the Yankee blue-belly paymaster."

"There's no sheriff or town marshal in Hell?"

"Shucks, no. It's a town for owlhoots to go to when things get hot. All you have to do is give the mayor ten percent of your loot and you can stop on and have a good time for as long as your money lasts."

"How is it that nobody's heard about Hell?" O'Day asked.

"It's been kept a secret," Dixon explained. "There's not

many folks go into the Palo Duro and the mayor makes sure only real owlhoots get through to the town."

"How does he do that?"

"He's got scouts up on the high points all 'round. They see somebody coming and light a fire. Ordinary folks see smoke up that ways, they steer well clear of it. Owlhoots, who know, head for it. Then one of the scouts meets you, takes all your guns, and shows you the way in."

"You mean that you fellers let him take *all* your weapons?" O'Day demanded.

"Them as didn't soon enough wished they had," Dixon elaborated. "If they didn't, the other scout signals and the Antelopes jumped 'em so fast they figured the hawgs'd come to feeding."

"So all I need to do is ride toward the Palo Duro country," O'Day commented, half to himself. "Head for the smoke and get guided into Hell. That sounds easy enough."

"It sure i—" Dixon agreed, then stared as the dude started to walk away. "Hey! Where're you headed?"

"To Hell," O'Day replied.

"How's about me?" Dixon yelped. "I've got this busted leg and can't travel on it."

"That's right," O'Day admitted. "You're not wanted any place?"

"Nope."

"And you don't have a price on your head?"

"Hell, no!"

"Then you're no use to me alive or dead," O'Day said quietly.

Drawing and cocking his Colt, O'Day shot Dixon in the head.

2

THAT WAS ONE MEAN TOWN

"What do you reckon's eating at Dusty, Lon?" Waco asked the Ysabel Kid as they stood clear of the laughing man and girls gathered around the campfire. "Something sure as hell is, and has been ever since we got clear of Hell."

Tall, slim, yet conveying an impression of possessing whipcord, untiring strength, the Kid had hair as black as a raven's wing and a deeply tanned face with handsome, almost babyishly innocent lines. Except, that is, for its red-hazel eyes. They warned that beneath the exterior lay a wild, reckless spirit. Instead of his usual all-black clothing, he wore a low-crowned, wide-brimmed J. B. Stetson hat of Texas style, fringed buckskin shirt, and Levi's jeans tucked into calf-high Comanche legging-moccasins. About his middle hung a gun belt, with a walnut-handled Colt 1848 Dragoon revolver butt forward in a low cavalry-twist draw holster on the right and an ivory-hilted James Black bowie knife sheathed at the left.

There was something suggestive of the Indian about the

Kid, which was hardly surprising. He had been born in the village of the *Pehnane*—Wasp, Raider, or Quick Stinger— Comanche band, maternal grandson of chief Long Walker and his French-Creole *pairaivo*.[1] His mother had died in childbirth and his father, a wild Irish-Kentuckian who had been adopted into the *Pehnane,* had often been away from the camp attending to the family businesses of mustanging and smuggling along the Rio Grande. So, in the traditional Comanche way, the Kid had been raised by his grandfather. That was no mean start in life. Long Walker was war leader of the Dog Soldier lodge and had been determined that his grandson would be worthy of acceptance into the exclusive brotherhood.

So the Kid had received a thorough schooling in all those matters a successful Dog Soldier must know.[2] Skill with weapons rated high on the curriculum. He had acquired considerable proficiency with bow and arrows, war lance, toma-hawk—and such expertise with a knife that he had earned the man-name *Cuchilo.* On obtaining the arms of his father's people, he had become adequate with the old Dragoon and almost unequaled in accurate shooting with a rifle. In the arts of horse management, trick riding, following tracks and hid-ing his own sign, locating hidden enemies or staying con-cealed when sought by keen-eyed hunters, he had graduated with honors.

It had not been an educational system calculated to endow its recipients with an exaggerated belief in the sanctity of human life. Nor had the Kid's formative years tended to increase his qualities in that field. When old enough, he had accompanied his father. By then Big Sam Ysabel had given up mustanging and was smuggling full time. So the youngster had been thrown into contact with some mighty tough, mean *hombres,* Texan and Mexican. The former had called him Sam Ysabel's kid at first, shortening it to the Ysabel Kid as he had come into greater prominence. Translating the name,

1. *Pairaivo:* chief and favorite wife.
2. Told in: *Comanche.*

the Mexicans had said *el Cabrito*. One thing all had been in agreement upon: Kid or old as sin, that Indian-dark, soft-spoken youngster was equal to anybody in tough, salty courage, and deadlier than most.

The war between the states had seen the Kid and his father employed as legal smugglers, delivering cargoes from Matamoros across the Rio Grande to the Confederate states' authorities. It had been tough and demanding work, carried out satisfactorily. With peace—or at least an end to open hostilities—the Ysabels had intended to go back to mustanging until more settled times made illegal smuggling profitable. Bushwhack lead had ended their hopes by cutting Big Sam down.

While hunting for his father's killers, the Kid had come to the turning point of his life. He had met and been helped by Dusty Fog, who was handling an assignment upon which the future peace of the United States had depended.[3] With both their missions concluded successfully, Dusty had offered to employ the Kid on the OD Connected ranch. Not as an ordinary hand, but to carry out scouting and similar duties as a member of the spread's floating outfit.

The great ranches often employed a floating outfit; half a dozen or so men who traveled the far ranges as a mobile crew, instead of being based at the main house. Ole Devil Hardin's floating outfit had also frequently found themselves dispatched to help their boss's friends out of difficulties and dangerous predicaments. In such tasks, the Kid's Comanche education had been of much use.

There were, the Kid had often mused, many points in common between himself and the youngster whose only name was Waco. And one difference. The Kid's life had been saved by Indians; Waco's parents had died by the same cause, although at the hands of the tribe from which he had taken his name. They were alike in that, but for meeting the Rio Hondo gun wizard, they might have now been riding the owlhoot trails with prices on their heads. Although the Kid

3. Told in: *The Ysabel Kid.*

had avoided it, there had always been the chance that he would run afoul of the law when smuggling. Waco's fall from grace would probably have been that he had killed too often and without reason.

Raised by a North Texas rancher with a large family, Waco had drifted away from them. As a tough youngster with a brace of fast guns, he had drawn the attention of Clay Allison. Always on the lookout for such talent, the Washita curly wolf had hired Waco to ride with his wild onion crew. It was not company in which a mild-mannered introvert could have survived, and it had left its mark. The youngster had become sullen, watchful, quick to take offense, because that was a good way to avoid being put upon.

So things had stood that day up in the Texas Panhandle, when Dusty Fog had saved Waco's life at some danger to his own. From the moment he had been set down, after Dusty had snatched him clear of the stampeding CA herd,[4] Waco had begun his redemption. At Dusty's request, Allison had let the youngster become a member of Ole Devil's floating outfit. In the company of men who had treated him like a favorite younger brother and were willing to explain things— which Allison's crew would never do—he had lost his ready aggression and learned much that would be of use to him in later years.

Most important of all, Waco had learned *when* to add to his knowledge of *how* to shoot.

Slightly taller than the Kid, with wider shoulders and a frame that told of developing strength and muscular power, Waco was dressed in expensive cowhand clothing. A white Stetson perched on his blond head at a jack-deuce angle over his right eye. Around his neck, a tight-rolled and knotted green silk bandana trailed its long ends down over a blue shirt. His jeans' cuffs hung outside high-heeled, fancy-stitched boots. Around his waist, a gun belt of exceptionally fine workmanship supported matched staghorn-handled 1860 Army Colts in contoured, tied-down holsters.

4. Told in: *Trigger Fast.*

Concern showed on his tanned, handsome young face as
he addressed the question to his older, more experienced
companion.

"You reckon so?" countered the Kid.

"I *know* so, you slit-eyed *Pehnane!*" Waco growled.

"There's some's'd say ole Dusty'd've been right pleased to
get out of it," the Kid drawled. "We had a good visit there,
we're coming back alive."

"Then what's—?"

"That was one mean town, boy, full of lousy folks."

"Why sure," Waco agreed, wondering if he could ever
cease being "boy" to the other members of the floating outfit. Not that he minded *them* calling him it, for their tones
always implied that he would, eventually, grow up into a
forty-four-caliber man.[5] "There wasn't a feller, nor woman,
in it that hadn't done real bad meanness one time or another."

"And we left them there," the Kid pointed out. "That's
what's eating at Dusty, boy. He left those folks, men and
women, in the Palo Duro, with the *Kweharehnuh* band all
'round them. Comes time for the bucks to collect their bullets and the folks can't hand 'em out, all hell's going to bust
loose in Hell."

"And serve them right, the stinking bastards. There's mur-
derers, cheats, thieves, and worse, 'n' nothing else but there.
They built the town, now let them pay for it."

"Dusty don't see it that way, boy."

"What we heard and saw of 'em," Waco protested, "they
can take care of themselves."

"Against things they know about, maybe," drawled the
Kid. "Only they're most all of them dudes. They don't know
sic 'em about Injuns and a whole heap less about riled-up
Antelope Comanches toting repeating rifles—"

"Which they've given to 'em," the blonde pointed out.

"I'm not gainsaying it," the Kid admitted. "And when

5. How the name came into being and what it implies is told in: *.44
Caliber Man.*

they handed those repeaters over, they made a promise.
When it's not kept, which it won't be, there'll be a whole
slew of riled-up bucks wanting to know why. Them's're
killed in the fighting'll be the lucky ones. And that goes
double for their womenfolk."

"What'll Dusty do?" Waco inquired, having no need to be
further enlightened upon the Comanches' treatment of white
female prisoners.

"Likely he'll tell us when he decides," the Kid replied.
"What do *you* reckon he'll do?"

"Go back to Hell and try to prize 'em loose," Waco
guessed. "Just's soon's we've delivered the money in the
wagon and seen the gals safe."

"Talking about the gals," the Kid said quietly, glancing at
the group about the fire. "How do you reckon they'll take it
when they learn who we are and that they're not going to get
any place close to as much of the money as they've been
counting on?"

"I'd say that all depends on how Emma takes it," Waco
guessed. "The rest'll go along with her. Happen they don't
cotton to the notion, we can count on Belle to back our play.
Anyways, once they learn we're not owlhoots, I reckon Hubert and the gals'll take what Dusty offers them. It'll be a fair
offer."

"Only not as much as they figured on getting," the Kid
reminded him.

"Things being how they are," Waco replied, "I'm betting
they'll take it."

Although the Kid would not have stated it so audibly, he
felt inclined to agree with his young *amigo*.

Despite what Dipper Dixon had told Break O'Day, the
town of Hell had not remained a complete secret. Jules Murat, captain of Texas Rangers, had learned enough to make
him suspect its existence. On being informed, the governor
had been faced with a problem. While determined to stamp
out lawlessness, and wishing to destroy a safe haven for
badly wanted men, Stanton Howard had no desire to pro-

voke an Indian war. Any attempts at the former, unless carefully handled, could easily have resulted in the latter.

Unlike the other bands of the Comanche Nation, the *Kwe-harehnuh* had refused to come to terms at the Fort Sorrell
peace treaty meeting.[6] Instead, they had retreated to their
wild, practically unexplored Palo Duro and Tule country to
follow the traditional *Nemenuh*[7] way of life. All the evidence
had pointed to the citizens of Hell having obtained permission to make their homes in the Palo Duro and immunity to
outlaws who wished to visit or leave the town. Part of the
payment for those privileges had been a repeating rifle and a
regular supply of ammunition for every war leader, *tehnap,*
and *tuivitsi* in the band.[8]

To send in the army would be inviting defeat, or an expensive, costly campaign against warriors fighting on their own
terrain. Before victory could be obtained, restless, unsettled
bravehearts on the reservations would have learned what
was happening and headed out to join the battle.

So Stanton Howard had decided that he must try to learn
just how dangerous the situation would be. Sending in Rangers posing as outlaws had not been practical. With so many
wanted men in the town, there would have been too great a
danger of the spies being recognized and exposed. What had
been needed were men of courage, initiative, and ability, but
who were not known to be connected with the forces of law
and order. They would also need an exceptional leader to
steer them through such a dangerous assignment.

With that latter qualification in mind, Governor Howard
had contacted Ole Devil Hardin and asked for the help of
the man he believed to be most suited to fill his needs: the
Rio Hondo gun wizard whose name was Dusty Fog.

People in Texas, never slow to praise their state's favorite
sons, had often claimed that Dusty Fog was the fastest, most

6. Why they did not is told in: *Sidewinder.*
7. *Nemenuh:* "The People," the Comanches' name for their nation.
8. *Tehnap:* an experienced warrior; *tuivitsi:* an adolescent, inexperienced
warrior.

accurate gun-handler in the West. It was also said that few
men could stand up against him in bare-handed fighting.
Those were qualities that he would need to stay alive in Hell,
but Howard had known there were others equally important.
In the governor's opinion, Dusty Fog had them all.

A captain in the Texas Light Cavalry at seventeen, Dusty
Fog had built a reputation as a military raider equal to that
of John Singleton Mosby or Turner Ashby. Ranging across
the less-publicized Arkansas battlefront, Dusty Fog had
played havoc with the Yankees.[9] It had been whispered how
he had supported Belle Boyd, the Rebel Spy,[10] on two of her
missions.[11] Less well known was how he had prevented two
fanatical Unionists from stirring up an Indian war that would
have decimated much of Texas.[12]

With the war over, and his uncle crippled in a riding acci-
dent,[13] Dusty had become segundo of the great OD Connected ranch. He had earned a name as a top hand with
cattle, a trail boss of considerable ability, and—although not
in Texas—had won acclaim as a capable town-taming peace
officer.[14] Small wonder that Stanton Howard had felt confident that Dusty could take on the assignment.

In accordance with a carefully formulated plan, Dusty, the
Kid, and Waco had gone to Hell. Their pose of being wanted
outlaws had been successful. So much so that they had completed their mission and, aided by Giselle Lampart, widow of
the mayor and founder of the town, lady outlaw Belle Starr,
and Emma Nene and some of her saloon's employees, they
had destroyed the *Kweharehnuh*'s next issue of ammunition
and brought away much of the citizens' ill-gotten gains.

9. Told in: *Under the Stars and Bars* and *Kill Dusty Fog!*
10. More of Belle Boyd's story is told in: *The Bloody Border, Back to the
Bloody Border, The Hooded Riders, The Bad Bunch,* and *The Whip and
the War Lance.*
11. Told in: *The Colt and the Sabre* and *The Rebel Spy.*
12. Told in: *The Devil Gun.*
13. Told in: "The Paint" episode of *The Fastest Gun in Texas.*
14. Told in: *Quiet Town, The Trouble Busters, The Making of a
Lawman, The Town Tamers,* and *The Small Texan.*

Up to that evening, only Belle Starr had known the trio's true identity, and she had good reasons for not exposing them. However, after three days of hard, fast traveling—at a camp set up close to the Swisher Creek some five miles from its junction with the Red River's Prairiedog Fork—Dusty had decided that the time had come to let the others of the party know where they stood. They had been under the impression that the money in their wagon was to be divided equally among them instead of being returned to the banks and stagecoach companies from which most of it had come.

"Well," drawled the Kid, nodding toward the gloomy outlines of the trees that surrounded the camp. "We'll right soon know what it's going to be."

Following the direction of his Indian-dark companion's gaze, Waco watched three figures take form and advance into the circle of firelight. Two were women with bodies and —in normal times—faces to catch the eye in any crowd. So far the various bruises gathered in the course of two long, grueling fights with each other had not faded away; but both Belle Starr and Emma Nene still showed sufficient traces of their matching, yet different beauties.

Currently Belle Starr's hair was dyed black. In three days she had managed to clear up the tangle in which it had been left by Emma's clutching fingers, as they had fought and provided a diversion while the other members of the party had stolen Mayor Lampart's loot. She wore a dark blue shirt, black riding breeches and high-heeled boots. A Manhattan Navy revolver swung in the fast-draw holster on her magnificently shaped right thigh. Her clothing showed off a body with rich, mature, and eye-catching curves.

Although a riding habit, open-necked blouse, and high-button shoes could not compete with Belle's attire for drawing male attention, Emma Nene had a figure every bit as voluptuous. She, too, had tidied up her blond hair, for she had no desire to be seen at a disadvantage by the man who strolled between them.

Going by her expression, Emma had just received a shock. Waco and the Kid could have guessed at what it had been.

Silence fell at the fire as Emma's big, burly bartender, Hubert, Giselle Lampart, and the six saloon girls stared in interest at the two women, but mainly at their escort. He was the man in whom Governor Stanton Howard had placed so much faith. A giant among his fellows as far as achievements were concerned.

From his low-crowned, wide-brimmed Texas-fashion Stetson to his high-heeled fancy-stitched boots, Dusty Fog measured a mere five foot six. He had curly, dusty-blond hair and a fairly handsome face that was unnoticeable when in repose. Only when he was roused did its full magnetism, strength of will, and the hint of intelligence beyond average make itself felt. Like his friends, he had played the part of an outlaw on a spree and purchased good clothes in Hell. He contrived to make them look like somebody's castoffs. Nor did the excellent gun belt and its twin bone-handled Colt Civilian Model Peacemakers in cross-draw holster appear to add anything to his stature.

In times of peace, Dusty Fog could have been overlooked as an insignificant nobody. That very rapidly changed when trouble reared its head.

"Dusty!" the Kid said quietly, forgetting for the first time since commencing with the deception to use the small Texan's assumed name. "There's riders coming!"

3
WE'LL SHOOT YOU WHERE
YOU STAND

"Who are they, Comanche?" Emma Nene asked, throwing a worried look around.

"Soldiers, sound of it," the Kid replied. "Ain't nobody else makes all that much clatter 'n' jingling."

"How many of them?" Dusty demanded, for he could only just make out the faint sound of hooves.

"Four, five maybe," estimated the Kid. "No more'n that, anyways."

"What color hosses're they on?" Waco challenged cheerfully.

Having brought their assignment to a successful conclusion, the youngster could see nothing to be concerned about from the presence of the soldiers.

"Have they seen us?" Hubert wanted to know, not sharing Waco's feelings on the subject.

"I'd say 'yes' to that," the Kid drawled. "Leastwise, they're headed right slap at us."

"What're we going to do?" yelped the pretty red-haired girl who had been Waco's escort in Hell.

"How's about you-all taking them on tooth 'n' claw, Red-gal," Waco suggested. "You can hold 'em off long enough for the rest of us to get away."

"Like hell I will!" the girl snorted. "Only I'd hate to have them find out what's in the wagon."

"And me!" Hubert agreed. "So how do we play it, Ed?"

"Make out you're a bunch of saloon folk headed for work in Colorado," Dusty decided. "You'd best hide in the wagon, Belle. Matt, Comanch', and me, we're cowhands stopping by for the night. Play it that way and everything'll be fine."

Even as he finished speaking, Dusty became aware of Emma Nene's eyes on him. There was more than a hint of suspicion in her scrutiny and he could guess at its cause. While walking with her and Belle, he had disclosed his true identity and made her an offer. In return for their help in Hell, Emma, Belle, and Giselle Lampart would each receive fifty thousand dollars. The rest of Emma's party were to be given ten thousand dollars apiece. That was less than any of them, with the exception of Belle, had anticipated; but it was backed by the small Texan's assurance that he would not mention their connection with the town. All in all, it was a generous offer.

Up to Dusty's speech, Emma had apparently been satisfied with the arrangement. Having seen the small Texan and his companions in action at Hell, she had known there was little her party could do other than accept. The three men and Belle Starr could nullify any protest. His words had created doubts. Instead of realizing that the subterfuge was for her and the other Hell's citizens' benefit, she had started to wonder if he really was Ed Caxton, wanted for murdering and robbing a U.S. Army paymaster.

There was no time for the small Texan to go into an explanation, even if—which he doubted—the blonde would be inclined to believe it. So he decided to say nothing further to Emma. In the interest of self-preservation, she would be unlikely to betray him.

Nearer came the sound of the hooves, mingled with the creaking of saddle leather and faint jingling of metal accoutrements that civilian travelers did not find necessary. Instinctively the Kid edged to where his Winchester Model 1866 rifle rested on the seat of the saddle he would be using as a pillow. Waco ambled across to stand alongside Dusty. Going to the wagon, Belle Starr swung herself onto its box and disappeared inside. The rest of the party remained around the fire.

"Hello, the camp!" bawled a voice. "U.S. Cavalry here. Can we come in?"

"Answer him, Hubert!" Dusty growled when the bartender looked for guidance. "It's you they'll expect it from."

"C-come ahead," the bartender replied.

Led by a tall, broad-shouldered young second lieutenant, a sergeant and three troopers rode from among the trees. They drew rein by the line of horses picketed on the fringe of the firelight and swung from their saddles. While the enlisted men stood by their mounts, the officer crossed to the fire. As he walked, his eyes darted from side to side and he seemed to be examining his surroundings with some care.

"My name's Kitson, Fourth Cavalry, ladies, gents," the officer introduced. "Is it all right if me and my men share your fire?"

"Feel free," Hubert offered, darting another look in Dusty's direction. "Coffee's on the boil and we're going to cook up supper."

"Thanks," Kitson answered, turning a quick glance in the direction the bartender had looked. "We didn't expect to meet anybody out this way."

"We've come up from Paducah," Hubert explained, selecting the only town he knew to be roughly south of their position. "Headed to work at the Bon Ton House in Denver."

"*All* of you?" queried the officer.

"These three young fellers met up with us around sundown," the bartender replied.

"We're on our way home from a trail drive, mister," Dusty

elaborated. "The folks were good enough to let us stay on here for the night."

"Uh-huh!" Kitson grunted in a matter-of-fact manner, as if three cowhands were beneath his serious notice. "I'll fetch my men along. I want to warn them about their behavior."

Swinging around, the officer strode away. Dusty watched him go, deciding that under the slightly pompous nature—which was only to be expected in a young second lieutenant—Kitson was most likely a capable soldier and popular leader. Certainly the enlisted men listened attentively to his low spoken words and showed no resentment, although they all had the appearance of long service.

After Kitson had finished speaking, each of the troopers unclipped his carbine from the leather sling draped diagonally over his left shoulder to the right hip. None of the Texans saw anything suspicious in the move. The carbine sling, a sixty-inch-long, three-inch-wide leather strap fitted with a polished steel ring and snap hook, had become a standard issue to the U.S. Cavalry during the war between the states. That had been brought about by the tendency of Union commanding officers to make their mounted men fight on foot. A combination of the sling and carbine ring had ensured that the weapon was always in its user's possession. However, the Springfield Model of 1870 carbine weighed seven pounds, fifteen ounces—no mean burden to have dangling at one's side. Experienced men would not leave their carbines on the slings in a friendly camp, but would pile them in a neat, easily separated pyramid close to the fire.

Fanning out in a casual-seeming manner, the soldiers walked toward the civilians. Suddenly, the troopers' carbines lifted and lined on the Texans. With fair speed, considering the awkward manner in which the United States' Army insisted that its personnel carry their revolvers, Kitson and his sergeant produced Colt Cavalry Peacemakers from their holsters.

"Don't move, or we'll shoot you where you stand!" Kitson

snapped, thumbing back the Colt's hammer and lining its muzzle on Dusty's chest.

"What—?" Hubert croaked, starting to rise.

"Don't be alarmed, sir," Kitson replied, without taking his attention from the small Texan. "Your visitors are our concern. They're Ed and Matt Caxton and the other one's name is Comanche Blood."

"Land sakes a-mercy!" Emma gasped, right hand fluttering to her mouth. "The men who robbed that paymaster and murdered all his men?"

"That's them, ma'am," the sergeant confirmed, and his revolver lined unerringly at the Kid. "Paddy Magoon was a good friend of mine."

Dusty could have cursed the unexpected turn of events. After leaving Hell, he and his *amigos* had shaved off the beards grown to lessen the chances of them being recognized. Unfortunately, the recognition had finally come from an entirely different source. That figured. Kitson had the look of a competent, efficient officer. So he would be unlikely to have forgotten the descriptions of the three men accused of robbing an army paymaster and murdering his whole escort. What was more, he had been smart enough to plan the best way in which to arrest the trio. When the story came out, a number of Yankee officers who had served in Arkansas were going to have red faces. None of them had come anywhere near to capturing Captain Dustine Edward Marsden Fog.

Apart from the embarrassment that would be caused for various officers, there was another and more immediate point to consider. How could Dusty, the Kid, and Waco evade capture without implicating Emma's party with the town of Hell? Or prevent Belle Starr from being arrested? Dusty had promised that his helpers would go free, without even being connected to the town, and he always believed in keeping his word.

One thing was for certain. Dusty knew that convincing Kitson of the truth would be anything but easy. The very nature of the deception had rendered impossible the carrying

of written proof of the trio's true identity. Angered at the
story that had been circulated, the soldiers would be unlikely
to accept the mere word of men they believed had cold-
bloodedly murdered several of their comrades in arms.

Unless, of course, they had no other choice but to accept.

Attaining that desirable situation would not be easy, if it
was to be done without the help of Hubert and the women.

"Let your gun belts fall," Kitson ordered. "Left-handed
and real slow."

"You've got us dead to rights, mister," Dusty drawled.
"Best we do what he says, boys."

"We can save a whole heap of fussing if we just shoot 'em
now," muttered the burly soldier covering Dusty.

"Shut off that kind of talk, Brill!" Kitson snapped. "I'll
have no more of it from you."

That removed one worry from Dusty's mind. No matter
what his personal feelings might be, the lieutenant did not
intend to carry out any private revenge on his captives. Nor
did he mean to let his escort do so. Although the other enlisted men showed their dislike of the trio, none of them
appeared to be openly supporting Brill's point of view.

Studying Brill, with eyes that read his character as if it had
been printed on his sullen face, Dusty decided that he would
offer the best opportunity to turn the tables on their captors.

Freeing the pigging thongs that held the tips of the holsters
to his thighs, Dusty unbuckled and lowered the gun belt to
his feet. All the time, he studied Brill with an infuriatingly
mocking sneer. He could see the soldier's indignation rising.
Which was just what the small Texan wanted to happen.

Waco and the Kid followed Dusty's example, satisfied that
he had some plan for their salvation in mind.

"Back away from the belts," Kitson commanded, as he
continued to advance with Brill at his side.

"Could be you're making a mistake, mister," Dusty remarked, standing his ground. "We don't know anything
about—"

"You heard the lieutenant!" Brill barked, delighted that
the short-grown son of a bitch had presented him with an

opportunity. Striding ahead of Kitson, he directed the muzzle of his Springfield in a savage thrust toward Dusty's midsection. "Move b—!"

Offered his chance, Dusty took it with devastating speed. In his eagerness to strike, Brill had inserted his big frame between the small Texan and the barrel of Kitson's revolver.

"Get out—!" the lieutenant bawled.

Like a flash, Dusty's right hand cupped under the Springfield's barrel and jerked it out of alignment. At the same moment, his left hand closed over the carbine's breech from above. Although Brill had involuntarily squeezed the trigger, the outside hammer was halted by the small Texan's hand before it could reach the head of the firing pin.

Finding his weapon grasped with surprising strength and turned from its target, Brill's first inclination was to reverse its direction. Instantly Dusty changed his twisting motion to the way in which the soldier intended it to go. Dusty's response took Brill by surprise. Pivoting slightly on his left foot, he plucked the carbine from the soldier's hands. Snapping it back, Dusty propelled the butt against the side of its owner's jaw and knocked him staggering.

Attracted by the commotion, the soldier covering Waco allowed his attention to wander. Watching the carbine swing toward Dusty, the youngster sprang forward. Taking his hold with both hands gripping from above, Waco felt the soldier trying to pull back from his grasp. Up swung the youngster's right foot to ram into the soldier's belly. Sinking into a sitting position, he dragged the trooper off balance. By rolling onto his back, pulling down with his hands and thrusting his foot upward, Waco caused his assailant to turn a half somersault through the air. With a startled yell, the trooper lost his hold on the carbine and landed upon his back beyond Waco's head.

Like Waco's watcher, the sergeant and third trooper heard the disturbance. They matched their companion's reaction in starting to turn away from their charge. Although the Kid immediately made his play, he was all too aware of the dangers doing so entailed. The non-com and the soldier were

experienced fighting men. So they had halted well beyond
the Kid's reach and sufficiently far apart for him to be unable
to launch a simultaneous attack on them. Any other way he
tried it would likely prove fatal for him.

However, the chance had to be taken. If not, either Dusty
or Waco would die. While one of them kept the Kid covered,
the other soldier would turn and shoot at their companions'
attackers. Sure enough, the sergeant was already swinging
his attention back to the Kid and the trooper made as if to
throw up and sight his carbine toward Dusty.

Cutting loose with a ringing *Pehnane* scalp-yell, the Kid
hurled himself into motion. He went forward in a swift dive,
aiming for the sergeant's legs. So swiftly did he move that he
passed under the barrel of the Colt as its wielder tried to
throw down on him. Enfolding his arms about the yellow-
striped blue breeches' knees, the Kid jerked them together
and heaved. Thrown off balance, the non-com sent a bullet
harmlessly into the air. Then his back smashed onto the
ground with enough force to jolt all the air from his lungs.
Wriggling forward with desperate speed, the Kid tried to
drop alongside the dazed non-com and use his body as a
shield. From the rapid way in which the third trooper was
turning and handling the Springfield, the Kid would not be
fast enough.

Having disposed of Brill, Dusty continued to move with
planned alacrity. He put himself in Kitson's place and decided that the officer would expect him to keep the trooper
between them. So he went the other way. That carried him in
the direction of the fire. Dusty was gambling on Kitson being
taken by surprise, but also that he would remain calm
enough to think.

Baffled by Dusty's actions, Kitson attempted to change his
point of aim. Instantly a difficulty arose. If he fired and
missed, his bullet would fly toward the—as he assumed—
innocent people around the fire. Rather than endanger the
women, the lieutenant was determined to be certain of
where his lead would end its flight.

With the Springfield lifting and lining at him, the Kid figured that his life expectancy was getting shorter by the second. The shot that cracked out did not come from any Army carbine. Struck on the foregrip by a bullet, the Springfield spun unfired from the trooper's hands. He gave a yelp of surprise and spun around to see who had intervened. Although his right hand was clawing at the flap of his revolver's holster, he refrained from completing the motion.

Standing inside the wagon, left knee bent and its foot resting on the back of the driver's seat, Belle Starr cradled the butt of her Winchester Model of 1866 carbine in the firing position. Smoke curled from its muzzle, which did not mean that it was now harmless. Unlike the single-shot Springfield issued to the cavalry, her weapon was a twelve-shot repeater. Down and up flicked her right hand, operating the loading lever that automatically ejected the empty case, cocked the hammer, and fed a live cartridge into the chamber. She made the movement with such deft ease that the Winchester .44/.28-caliber barrel never wavered in its alignment on the soldier's chest.

Belle had guessed at Dusty's predicament, and so had been prepared to lend a hand at the opportune moment. Collecting her carbine from the wagon, she had remained concealed and cut in most effectively to save the Kid's life.

Throwing a grateful glance at his rescuer, the Kid rolled from the sergeant and snatched up the other's discarded Peacemaker. Usually the Indian-dark Texan professed to despise the new metallic-cartridge Colt, but he admitted silently that one of them could feel right comforting to a man's hand given the correct conditions.

Advancing slightly to the right of Kitson, Dusty raised the borrowed carbine vertically and flung it at him. It struck the officer's gun wrist with numbing force. Deflected aside and downward, the Colt cracked. Dirt erupted a few feet from Kitson's feet as the bullet plowed in. Giving the officer no time to recover, Dusty changed direction. Gliding in, he clamped both hands onto Kitson's right wrist. Carrying the trapped limb into the air, Dusty pivoted below it and snapped it downward sharply. Unable to help himself, Kitson felt his feet leave the ground. Turning upside down in mid-flight, he landed rump-first and lost his hold on the revolver. Releasing his grip, Dusty scooped up the Colt. Cocking its hammer, he turned to see if his *amigos* required assistance.

Going by all appearances, the Kid and Waco had contrived to deal with their share of the soldiers and were unharmed. The blond youngster was sitting up and lowering the carbine he had been lining on Kitson. Knowing Waco's sense of loyalty, Dusty figured that the lieutenant had come mighty close to being shot. Beyond a scared-looking trooper and recumbent sergeant, the Kid was rising. He looked a mite guilty as he noticed Dusty's pointed glance at the long-barreled Peacemaker in his hand.

"I figured it'd make a good club," the Kid excused himself.

"Most times he wouldn't even say that." Waco grinned, following the direction of Dusty's gaze and guessing what had prompted the Kid's comment.

From his companions, Dusty turned his attention to the rest of the camp. Giving a grateful nod to Belle in passing, he studied the people from Hell. Emma Nene's face showed a mixture of disappointment and relief. All the saloon girls had stood up and none hid her pleasure at seeing that the three Texans were back in control of the situation. Worry etched lines on Hubert's face as he waited to see how the "Caxton brothers" and "Comanche Blood" would deal with the soldiers. By all accounts, they had wiped out a colonel and his escort to steal a payroll. So they would be unlikely to let the cavalrymen survive. Smarter than the girls, Hubert could foresee bad trouble ahead if the lieutenant and his men were murdered. Yet he knew of no way that he could prevent it happening.

Only Giselle Lampart appeared unmoved, either by the Texans' escape or over the soldiers' possible fate. Small, brunette, with a beautiful, vivacious face, she wore a gingham dress that suggested her figure would have matched that of Belle or Emma if she had been their height. Her eyes darted around in an inquisitive manner and Dusty sensed that she was waiting eagerly for him to order the cavalrymen's deaths.

"Well!" Kitson gritted, rising to face Dusty. "Get on with it, you murdering son of a bitch."

"Like I said," the small Texan replied, accepting the insult as having been spoken by a man under great stress. "Could be you've made a mistake."

Shaking his head to clear it, Brill swung toward Dusty. Hate blazed on the soldier's face. Unmindful of the revolver in the small Texan's hand, the surly trooper clawed open his holster. Something hissed viciously through the air. A screech burst from Brill's lips and, forgetting the weapon he had meant to draw, his hands clutched wildly at the feathered shaft of an arrow that had penetrated his chest so deeply that its barbed head had emerged at the back.

War whoops shattered the night and several *Kweharehnuh* Comanche warriors burst into the firelight from all sides of the camp.

4

GET THE WHITE WITCH!

The attack was launched with typical *Nemenuh* speed, savagery, and deadly intent. While there was not time for an accurate trail count, the Kid figured that at least two dozen assorted *tehnaps* and *tuivitsis* were boiling out from the places of concealment they had selected in a circle around the clearing. He noticed other things, his mind ticking them off automatically even as he prepared to defend himself.

Despite most of the Comanches' clothing having been made from the hides of pronghorn antelopes, which labeled them as *Kweharehnuh* to the Kid's eyes, only a few braves carried firearms. That fact gave the Kid less comfort or satisfaction than might have been expected. He knew that the people of Hell had presented every *Kweharehnuh* warrior with a repeating rifle or carbine and a regular supply of ammunition to go with it. If some of the attackers—the majority in fact—had elected to lay aside their Winchesters or Spencers, it was because they intended to count coup by personal

contact. Doing so rated far higher in a Comanche's estimation than when one was claimed after standing back to take
an enemy's life with a bullet or an arrow.

No matter what kind of weapons they were carrying, the
braves displayed a mutually determined eagerness to come
to grips with the hated white people around the campfire.

Screams of fright broke from the saloon girls. Instead of
acting in a sensible manner, five of the six scattered wildly
like chickens spooked by a diving Cooper's hawk. Acting in
blind panic, the Mexican girl who had been assigned to keep
the Kid company in Hell ran straight to her death. A grizzled
tehnap rammed his war lance into her body and gutted her
with casual, deft ease.

Clenching her fists like a male pugilist, Emma Nene stood
her ground. Letting out a screech, Giselle Lampart buckled
at the knees and sank to crouch motionless. With his right
hand fanning toward the butt of his holstered Colt, Hubert
started to move in his employer's direction. While scared,
Red showed a better grasp of the situation than her fellow
workers. Instead of fleeing blindly, she darted rapidly in
search of Waco's protection.

Lurching into a sitting position, the sergeant grabbed instinctively at his empty holster. An expression of horror
creased his leathery face as he realized that he was unarmed.
Deprived of his carbine by Belle's bullet, the second of the
Kid's would-be captors tried to draw his revolver. Shooting
on the run, one of the firearm-toting minority sent a Spencer
bullet into the soldier's head.

Disturbed by the sudden commotion, the horses bucked,
reared, snorted, and generally displayed their disapproval.
The animals owned by Dusty's party had been secured to a
stout picket line and it held firm against their struggles. Having been eager to arrest the three "outlaws," Kitson had
ordered his men to leave their horses with the reins trailing.
Normally that would have kept the well-trained remounts
motionless. Fright overrode training and the cavalry horses
went bounding into the darkness.

Not one of the braves gave the departing horses as much

as a glance, although any of the animals would have been a valuable piece of booty.

Taking in the precarious nature of their situation with a swift glance, Dusty Fog responded with his usual speed. He held Lieutenant Kitson's revolver and so had the means to protect himself—but the officer was unarmed and would rate high on the attackers' list of victims.

"Here, mister!" Dusty snapped, and tossed the long-barreled Cavalry Model Peacemaker to Kitson.

Although startled and puzzled by such an action from a man he believed to be a cold-blooded killer, the officer grabbed for and caught the weapon around its frame. He transferred his right hand to the walnut handle and prepared to sell his life dearly.

Having provided the officer with the means of self-preservation, Dusty gave thought to obtaining the same for himself. Turning, he hurtled through the air in a rolling dive toward his own weapons. Even as he went down, he saw a wild-eyed *tuivitsi* rushing in his direction and holding a razor-sharp, spear-pointed war lance ready to strike.

Hitting the ground on his left side and with his back to the lance carrier, Dusty closed his fingers around the matched Colts' bone grips. Rolling to face his assailant as the lance rose high to gain impetus for its thrust, Dusty flung aside the gun belt and freed the four-and-three-quarter-inch barrels from the holsters. Thumb-cocking the hammers while lying flat on his back, Dusty angled the guns upward to where the brave was preparing to drive home the lance. Both revolvers spat at the same moment. Struck in the center of the chest, the *tuivitsi* was flung backward and down.

Hearing Red's scream as he bounded to his feet, Waco swung his gaze in search of her. What he saw brought an instant response. A pursuing warrior had caught up with the girl, gripped her by the hair, and was dragging her backward. Up swung the brave's tomahawk as the girl toppled to the rear. Waco flung the acquired Springfield to the aim and squeezed its trigger. With the back of his skull shattered where the bullet had burst out, the *Kweharehnuh* released the girl's hair and collapsed. Rolling onto her hands and knees with frantic haste, Red looked back at her attacker. Letting out a shriek, she flopped face forward in a faint.

There was no time for Waco to display concern over Red's indisposition. He held an empty weapon, for which he possessed no ammunition. *That* was not a good way to be situated under the circumstances. Tossing the Springfield aside, he darted to where he had laid down his gun belt.

Believing that he had caused the blond ride-plenty's flight, a whooping young *tuivitsi* gave chase. Waco heard the rapidly approaching thud of feet and spun to face his pursuer. Around swung the *tuivitsi*'s tomahawk in a horizontal slash aimed at taking the blonde's head from his shoulders. In his inexperience, the brave was overconfident. So he was taken by surprise by his would-be victim's rapid and unexpected response.

Instead of standing petrified until killed, Waco ducked under the blow. Still crouching, he lunged and butted his skull into the *tuivitsi*'s belly. As breath belched from the Comanche's lungs, the blonde wrapped both arms about his bare thighs. Straightening up suddenly, Waco raised the *tuivitsi* and released his hold at the height of the other's elevation. Expecting the Indian to crash helplessly, Waco once more turned and sprang toward his gun belt.

Trained almost from birth to ride bucking horses, including numerous lessons in how to fall off without being injured, the *tuivitsi* contrived to light down on his feet. The impetus of the throw caused him to run forward several steps, but he retained his grip on the tomahawk's handle. Twirling around, he charged once more at the Texan.

Snatching out his right-hand Colt in passing, Waco pivoted to meet the attack. The *tuivitsi* was closing fast and with a fanatical determination that would not be halted by less than death. There was neither the time nor the need for Waco to take a careful aim. Assuming a crouching posture, with his right elbow locked tight against his side, Waco flashed across his left hand to draw back and release the hammer. Three times, so fast that the shots could hardly be detected as separate sounds, Waco made the fanning motion. Each .44 bullet plowed into the *tuivitsi*'s torso and turned his advance into a reeling, uncontrolled retreat.

Before Hubert could complete his draw, he was impaled by an arrow. Running past the front end of the wagon, a stocky war-bonnet chief nocked another arrow to the string of the bow he carried.

"Get the white witch!" he roared, starting to raise the arrow in Emma Nene's direction.

Hearing and understanding the words, taken with the sight of the chief's obvious interest in Emma, Belle lined her carbine. It barked and the flat-nosed bullet passed between the trailing ends of the headdress to shatter the man's spinal column. He went down with his bow still undrawn.

"He's sure got old Emma's character off well," Belle mused as she threw the carbine's lever through its reloading cycle.

A harsh ripping sound from behind caused Belle to spin around. Although the visibility inside the wagon was poor, she could make out that its closed, fastened rear flaps were shaking violently. Guessing that a Comanche was trying to gain access, she was faced with the problem of how to stop him. Then she saw a dull glitter as a knife's blade pierced the canvas. Four times, as fast as she could work the lever and squeeze the trigger, muzzle blasts illuminated the interior. Holes appeared in a vertical line across the flaps above the knife. A scream of pain followed the third shot. The knife was withdrawn suddenly. Its departure was followed by a thud and violent thrashing sound. Belle decided that these had been caused by the intruder falling and making violent, convulsive motions in his agony.

Satisfied that she had nothing further to fear from that direction, Belle swiveled once more to the open end of the canopy. Partially dazzled by the flashes of burning powder erupting from the carbine's muzzle, she saw a brave had caught Emma by the arm. Instead of striking the blonde down, he thrust her from him and sprang toward the crouching figure of Giselle Lampart.

Belle snapped off a shot that missed, due to the brave bending and taking hold of the brunette's left arm. Jerking down the lever, the lady outlaw felt something snap inside the carbine. Instead of completing its various reloading functions, the mechanism stayed stubbornly open. Having experienced such a sensation on another—although less demanding—occasion, Belle knew that one of the toggle links had broken. It was a defect that plagued the earlier models of Winchester.[1]

Cursing furiously, Belle dropped the useless carbine. Down dipped her right hand and drew the Manhattan Navy revolver from its contoured holster. Then she prepared to spring from the wagon and move to a distance at which she might hope to hit something with the handgun.

Like Dusty, the Kid did not leave a soldier defenseless against the attackers. Dropping the revolver into the sergeant's lap, he leapt to retrieve his own rifle. A brave, taller and slimmer than most *Nemenuh,* came leaping to intercept the Kid with a tomahawk lifting ready to hurl into flesh.

Gathering up the Winchester, with his right hand grasping the foregrip, the Kid slid his left forefinger into the trigger guard and the other three through the lever's ring. Raising the rifle to waist level, he shot the brave with the muzzle not three feet from the other's bare chest. Already the tomahawk had commenced its downward swing. Sidestepping as soon as he had squeezed the trigger, the Kid heard the hiss as the blade passed his sleeve harmlessly. Then he saw something that demanded his immediate and undivided attention.

Grasping an arm each, two *Kweharehnuh tehnap* were dragging Giselle Lampart away from the campfire. Even as the Kid snapped the Winchester's butt to his shoulder, knowing that shooting from the hip would not serve his needs, he felt puzzled. Not by the attempted abduction; a white woman made an acceptable piece of loot, almost as useful as a mule, but not so valuable as a horse or a gun. So he was not sur-

1. A more detailed description of this defect is given in: *Calamity Spells Trouble.*

prised to see the braves attempting to take the brunette with them.

What aroused the Kid's curiosity was their reason for having run straight past a saloon girl and for shoving Emma Nene aside when both were larger, stronger, and therefore more desirable as work-producing captives than the diminutive Giselle would be.

There was no time for the Kid to debate the problem. If he hoped to save Giselle from a fate worse than death, he had to concentrate. Sighting the Winchester, he shot the brave to the brunette's left in the head. Smoothly altering his point of aim as he flickered the lever up and down, he tumbled her second abductor in a lifeless heap. Shrieking hysterically, Giselle crumpled between the two dead *tehnap*.

Much to the Kid's further puzzlement, a leathery-faced *tehnap*, who had been bending to take Hubert's revolver from its holster, dropped the weapon. Yelling an order to the nearest *tuivitsi*, the old warrior discarded his trophy and ran to Giselle's side. Jerking his lance from the body of the saloon girl he had impaled, the *tuivitsi* darted to join the *tehnap*. Neither of them offered to use his weapon on the small woman, but bent to grab her by the ankles. With their holds obtained, they headed toward the trees.

The Kid shot the *tehnap* in the head, figuring him to have posed the greater threat to the brunette. Even as the Winchester started to turn, Dusty's, Waco's, and Kitson's revolvers thundered and all three bullets found their mark in the *tuivitsi*'s vital areas. Spinning around, the dying brave crashed across Giselle's flaccid body.

Then, with the same abruptness that had marked their arrival, the remainder of the Comanches fled. They darted swiftly into the darkness from which they had erupted not five minutes earlier and were gone from sight. Four of the saloon girls, Hubert, two soldiers, and ten Comanches lay dead or dying.

Screaming hysterically, Giselle Lampart was trying to wriggle from beneath the *tuivitsi*'s body. Having come within inches of being shoved into the fire, Emma Nene staggered clear of the flames. Covering her face with her hands, she sank to her knees and sobs shook her. Belle dropped from the wagon and moved cautiously toward the blonde. Regardless of the Manhattan in the lady outlaw's hand, the second living saloon girl dashed into her arms and clung on hysterically. On her hands and knees again, Red was shuddering and backing away from the body of her assailant.

At the first hint that the badly mauled *Kweharehnuh* were calling off their attack, the Kid had swiveled around and slanted his Winchester ready to cover the horses at the picket line. To his amazement, not one of the departing braves made any attempt to approach the restless animals. The omission merely added a further puzzling aspect to the various unusual actions of the attackers.

The Kid did not for a moment imagine that the *Kweharehnuh* braves were fleeing in panic. They had gone because they had seen that the attack was becoming a costly failure. Brave as they undoubtedly were, the Antelopes would not throw their lives away uselessly on a doomed project when they could escape. Nor would a *Nemenuh* braveheart, forced to retreat, pass up an opportunity to regain something of his lost honor.

So why had the departing warriors ignored the line of horses?

Maybe the whole bunch could not be liberated simultaneously; but any *tuivitsi* old enough to follow his first war trail should have been able to cut loose, mount, and ride away on one of the horses.

Yet none of them had offered to do so.

It was baffling behavior, completely unlike anything the Kid would have expected from Comanches in general and *Kweharehnuh*—who he admitted to be near on as good warriors as the *Pehnane*—in particular. By birth, training, and natural inclination, the Kid had developed a dislike for unsolved mysteries.

There could be an explanation to the departure without acquiring the horses. The braves might be planning to regroup and launch another attack. Not a likely contingency,

but possible in view of so many departures from normal Comanche behavior.

Usually night was a time for undetected traveling, raiding
—called horse stealing by people who did not belong to the
Nemenuh—but not for making war. Of course, presented
with a suitable opportunity, the chance to count coups and
gather loot would cause warriors to fight during the dark
hours. After losing so many companions, that particular war
party would be regretting its decision and was unlikely to
return.

Or would be unlikely, *if* they were acting like typical members of the Comanche Nation.

"Watch out in case they come back, Dusty!" called the
Kid, lowering his rifle and bounding across the clearing. "I'll
see what they're doing."

"Bueno," the small Texan replied. "Waco, tend to the
horses before we lose some of them."

"It's done," the youngster answered, thrusting the Colt
into his waistband and running to obey.

Lowering his smoking Peacemaker, Kitson turned slowly
and looked around. His eyes flickered from Brill to the second dead soldier, then moved on to where Waco's "watcher"
was sitting up and shaking his head in a dazed manner. The
sergeant was rising, also studying the situation.

"Are you all right, Tebs?" Kitson demanded.

"Huh?" grunted the soldier, gazing around with growing
awareness of what he was seeing. "What—what's happened?"

"He was down all through the fight, sir," the sergeant
commented, holstering his revolver. "Come out of it better'n
Chiano and Brill, they've both cashed in."

"Did they get you, sergeant?" the lieutenant inquired.

"Nope," admitted the non-com and nodded to one of the
dead *Kweharehnuh*. "He would've if that Blood feller hadn't
given me back my gun."

Hearing the words reminded the young officer that he,
too, had been saved by the return of his revolver. They also
brought back to him a recollection of why he had been point-

ing it at his rescuer. If that damned troublemaker Brill had not acted in such a stupid manner, there would have been no need for Kitson to lose his Colt—or to be in debt to a man who he must now arrest, take in, and most likely cause to be hanged.

Well, Brill was beyond any reproach for his actions. That left the small Texan. Kitson sucked in a breath, squared his shoulders, and turned with the intention of doing his duty.

Two Civilian Model Peacemakers lined their .45-caliber muzzles directly at the lieutenant's stomach, hammers back at full cock and forefingers resting lightly on the triggers. Unnoticed, the small Texan had got up and was ready to resist being arrested.

"Just holster your gun, mister," Dusty requested. "Leave yours be, sergeant, and have your trooper do the same."

"Keep your hand offen it, Tebs!" growled the non-com as the soldier grabbed toward his holster. "He could drop Mr. Kitson before you clear leather."

"I can't let you ride off, even though you saved my life," Kitson warned, showing no inclination to do as Dusty had suggested.

"All I'm wanting is a chance to talk," the small Texan drawled. He twirled his Colts around, allowing the hammers to sink without setting off the waiting powder charges, and returned them to their holsters. "Maybe this'll show you that I'm not asking for anything else."

"You've got nothing to lose by listening, Mr. Kitson," the sergeant remarked politely. "They could've let us get killed, but they didn't."

"They maybe figured we'd be more use alive than dead right then," Kitson pointed out. "Well, my grandfather always use to say that nobody was ever a loser by listening. Talk ahead, Mr. Caxton."

"First off, mister," Dusty said, "I'd sooner you called me by my real name."

"What would that be?" Kitson inquired.

"Dusty Fog," the small Texan replied.

5

THEY CAME TO TAKE
GISELLE

"Dusty Fog!"

Two startled voices repeated the name as the officer and sergeant exchanged glances. Then they swung mutually disbelieving gazes in the small Texan's direction, subjecting him to a long, hard scrutiny.

"What I'd heard," the sergeant declared, "was that you was with Governor Howard meeting some other ranchers down to San Antone, *Cap'n Fog.*"

"That's just what the *Texas State Gazette* said," Dusty admitted, feeling no annoyance at the soldiers' reactions. Few people could reconcile his appearance with his reputation, until they had come to know him. "What the Ysabel Kid, Waco, and I've been doing, it helped that everybody thought that's where we were at."

To assist in the deception they had practiced upon the citizens of Hell, Dusty had arranged for a story to appear in the *Texas State Gazette* and other newspapers. It had told of protests by various ranchers at a beef contract awarded to the OD connected, and how the governor had called the affected parties to a meeting in San Antonio de Bexar in the hope of averting a range war. He had sent Mark Counter,[1] another member of the floating outfit, to the town posing as himself. Six foot three in height, magnificently built, blond-haired, and exceptionally handsome, Mark had the kind of physical attributes most people expected of a man with Dusty Fog's reputation. The blond giant had been mistaken for Dusty enough times to give the subterfuge a chance of working.

"And where were you?" Kitson wanted to know.

"You said that Paddy Magoon's your friend, sergeant," Dusty remarked, without answering the question.

"He was," the non-com growled bitterly. "I should have a hundred dollars for every drink we've took together."

"Knowing him like you must," Dusty went on, "do you think he'd sell out the army and take up with a bunch of owlhoots who were fixing to kill and rob other soldiers?"

"I'd've staked my life he wouldn't," the sergeant declared. "Like I said, he was a damned good friend."

"He won't be when he hears that you aim to toss me in the pokey for *not* having killed him." Dusty grinned. "Because that's just the kind of mean lie I aim to tell him."

"Tell . . . ?" repeated the sergeant. "You mean he's still alive?"

"He is, unless he's been killed off by eating civilian cooking down to the OD Connected," Dusty confirmed. "Because that's where Paddy, Colonel Stegg, and the rest of our 'victims' are right now."

"You're saying that there's no truth in the stories about y—the robbery and killings?" Kitson demanded.

"No more than in the ones about Wyatt Earp being a fine, honest, upstanding Kansas lawman," Dusty agreed. "It was all done for a purpose."

1. Mark Counter's history is told in other of the author's floating outfit novels.

"The editors of all those newspapers deliberately lied?"

"Most of them just copied what the editor of the *Texas State Gazette* printed, mister."

"But he agreed to lie?" Kitson insisted.

"He was asked by the governor if he'd do it," Dusty explained and grinned. "On top of which, he rode in my company during the war and figured he'd best do me a li'l favor."

"And what was it all in aid of?" Kitson asked, but he still kept his Colt in his hand.

"To help us stay alive while we were carrying out a confidential assignment for Governor Howard *and* the United States Cavalry," Dusty replied. "I can't tell you more than it took us into the Palo Duro—"

"That's *Kweharehnuh* country!" the lieutenant exclaimed, looking at the body of the nearest Comanche.

"Like you say," Dusty drawled. "That's *Kweharehnuh* country. I can't tell you any more about what we were doing, though. And I can't come out with anything to prove I'm speaking the truth. We couldn't carry anything that might show who we really are."

All the time they had been speaking, Kitson was studying Dusty carefully. The lieutenant had noticed that the small Texan's gray eyes met his without flinching and how he answered every question instantly. There was nothing evasive or furtive in his demeanor that hinted he might not be speaking the truth.

Yet could that short, insignificant-looking Texas cowhand really be the almost legendary Dusty Fog?

Kitson knew of Dusty's Civil War reputation, as a courageous, gallant, and capable cavalry leader. There had been other stories told since peace had come, impressive enough individually or as a whole. They had not concerned the deeds of a small, almost inconspicuous man.

Fresher in the lieutenant's mind was the memory of how swiftly Dusty had moved when presented with the opportunity to evade arrest. Or of how the Texan had behaved following his taking of the chance. He had come into possession of a weapon with which to shoot Kitson if he had been so minded. Instead, at some considerable danger to himself, he had been content merely to disarm the officer. That had hardly been the act of a cold-blooded killer in a desperate bid for freedom.

During the conversation, Kitson had repeatedly found himself forgetting that he addressed a small, none-too-noticeable Texas cowhand. Instead he had begun to regard Dusty as a real big man with an air of command and leadership in his voice and attitude. The small Texan spoke with the accent of a well-educated Southerner; but that in itself was not a definite sign of innocence. Too many of them had been driven into a life of crime by the injustices of the Reconstruction period.

Kitson was a career officer and as such had developed the ability to judge men's characters with some accuracy. Continuing his scrutiny of the small Texan, he reached a conclusion. Unlikely as it seemed, he believed that he had been hearing the truth.

"It's a strange story," Kitson declared, after a lengthy pause for thought. "If you was Ed Caxton, you'd have thought up something a whole heap more likely than that."

"Why didn't you tell us this from the start?" the sergeant wanted to know.

"Would you have listened if I'd tried right then?" Dusty countered.

"Probably we wouldn't," Kitson conceded, and finally replaced his Peacemaker in the high-riding cavalry-twist hand holster. "I'll accept your story, Captain Fog, but I hope you'll not take offense if I talk to your two men?"

"Feel free," Dusty offered. "Only I reckon it can wait until we've got these folks settled down a mite."

"Hey now!" the sergeant put in, ogling Belle Starr as she and Emma, having dragged aside the dead Comanche, tried to calm Giselle down. "Who's she? That's no calico queen."

"You're right, soldier," Dusty agreed, then decided to become evasive. "I reckon you've heard of Belle Boyd?"

"The Rebel Spy?" the non-com asked. "I'll say I have. Is that her?"

"Belle's been helping us on the assignment," Dusty stated truthfully, without directly confirming or denying the sergeant's question. He saw a way out of a difficulty, providing the soldiers accepted the lady outlaw's borrowed identity. "Only her part's not finished yet."

"If there's anything I can do to help Miss Boyd—" Kitson began.

"There just might be at that," Dusty drawled. "Right now, though, those other folk could use our help."

"They can," the officer admitted, and his eyes flickered to the dead soldiers. "Damn it to hell! I've lost two of my men."

"It happens, mister," the small Texan replied gently. "But a good officer never stops feeling bad when it does. If you want to tend to them, Waco and I'll do what we can for the women."

In addition to wanting to help the lieutenant get over the loss of the two men, Dusty had no wish for him to make too close a scrutiny of the women. If he did, he might draw the correct conclusions from Belle's and Emma's bruised and fight-marked faces.

Leaving the soldiers, Dusty went to help Red rise. The girl was shaking with mingled emotions, but calmed down when he assured her everything was going to be all right.

"Wh-what about them?" Red inquired in a whisper, nodding to Kitson and the sergeant. "Aren't they going to arrest you?"

"Nope," Dusty replied. "I've got everything straightened out. Just keep quiet and Emma will tell you everything."

Escorting the saloon girl to join the other women, Dusty had no time to do more than ask if anything could be done for Hubert and the other casualties when the Kid returned. The dark Texan led Kitson's and another of the cavalrymen's horses.

"They've gone, Dusty, and aren't likely to be coming back," the Kid announced. "How come the blue-bellies don't have you hawg-tied?"

"I've told them who we are," Dusty replied.

"They believe it?"

"Sure, but they still wanted to jail *you* when I let on what your right name is."

"I'm not surprised, company I keep," the Kid sniffed and became serious. "How much did you tell?"

"Who we are, where we've been, but nothing about Hell," Dusty answered. "I don't reckon you'll need to tell him more than that. Unless either of them asks who Belle is . . ."

"And then?" the Kid prompted.

"Make them think she's Belle Boyd."

"You mean *lie* to 'em?"

"Let the white half do it, if the Comanche in you won't," Dusty suggested. "Or sort of make out she's the Rebel Spy without coming flat-footed and saying it's so. That should ease what passes for your conscience."

"Count on it," grinned the Kid, although he was not entirely sure what a conscience might be. "I'll go give the shavetail his hoss back. That ought to put me in good with him."

"It's long gone time when you was in good with somebody," Dusty grunted. "Something bothering you, Lon?"

"Sure. I'm thinking about why those *Kweharehnuh* jumped us."

"After loot, way you've always talked about things like this."

"Not this time. They lit out without taking a hoss, and I saw one *tehnap* drop Hubert's handgun without being shot nor bothered by us."

"So what do you reckon?" Dusty demanded.

"It's just a notion, mind," the Kid replied quietly. "But I think they came to take Giselle there back to Hell."

"You've got more than a notion on it," Dusty guessed.

"Plenty more," the Kid confirmed. "I saw enough— The shavetail's headed this way."

"Go and get in good with him," Dusty ordered. "And mind what I told you to tell him."

Leaving the Kid to hand over the horses and answer Kitson's questions, Dusty turned his attention to the women.

Belle and Emma had taken Giselle to sit by the wagon and left Red to care for her. They looked from Dusty to the soldiers and back.

"I was hoping to see you get arrested, Dusty." Belle smiled. "Isn't that shavetail going to?"

"Nope," Dusty answered. "Neither you nor me, Miss Boyd."

"Boyd?" Belle repeated, then a flicker of understanding crossed her face. "You've told them that I'm the Rebel Spy?"

"Would I lie?" Dusty grinned. "Let's just say that I've planted that same notion in his head."

"And how about *us,* E- . . . Dus- . . . Captain Fog?" Emma demanded.

"Try saying 'Dusty,'" the small Texan suggested. "You'll be all right. Maybe you won't be headed direct to Denver, but Lieutenant Kitson will see you safe to the nearest town."

"What about you?" Emma asked and nodded to the wagon. "And it?"

"I'll give you ladies your cut before we split up," Dusty promised. "And see that you get to wherever you want to go without anybody knowing you've come from Hell."

"But where are *you* going?" Emma insisted.

"Back there," Dusty replied. "If what Lon's told me is right, I have to get back to Hell as soon as I can."

"Why, Dusty?" Belle gasped.

"They're not going to stand up and cheer when you get there," Emma warned, but there was a calculating glint in her eyes as she studied the small Texan.

"Maybe they will," Dusty said quietly. "For the same reason that Simmy Lampart liked having me around."

"Because you're good with your guns," Belle guessed, then stiffened slightly. "Dusty! You think the *Kweharehnuh* are going to jump the town?"

"It's likely," Dusty admitted.

"We all knew *that* would happen before we left," Emma sniffed, and there was a hint of suspicion in her tone for which neither Dusty nor Belle could account. "Why're you bothered about it so suddenly?"

"Because I hoped we'd see you safe and get to Wichita Falls, then telegraph for the army to move in before it happened," Dusty explained. "Only, if Lon's calling the play correct, things're due to pop wide open before they could get to Hell and fetch the folks out."

"I *knew* something had been sticking in your craw ever since we pulled out," Belle declared. "And, if I'd been in better shape, I'd have seen what it was."

"What?" Emma challenged.

"Leaving those folks behind at the mercy of the *Kweharehnuh*," Belle told her. "Dusty doesn't think he's done the right thing by them."

"You're worried about the kind of folks there're in Hell?" the blonde asked, showing even more suspicion.

"Maybe you couldn't understand that—" Belle began.

"Lon figures the *Kweharehnuh* who hit us just now were trying to grab Giselle and take her back with them," Dusty remarked, before Emma could make an angry response to the lady outlaw's words.

"Why Giselle?" Emma inquired, curious enough to forget her annoyance.

"Because she's the one who used to help Simmy make his 'medicine' to guard the ammunition," Dusty replied.

"Hey!" Belle exclaimed. "That war-bonnet chief said something about grabbing the white witch, but I thought he meant—"

"Who did you think he meant?" the blonde bristled, having already formed her own conclusion.

"He said that, huh?" Dusty drawled, once more pouring oil on troubled waters before anything could flare up between the women.

"Maybe not in those exact words, but close enough to them," Belle answered. "I understand enough Comanche to get his meaning. He said for his men to grab the white witch."

"What use would Giselle be to them without Simmy to saw her in half?" Emma wanted to know.

A former stage magician, Mayor Simeon Lampart had made use of his talents to impress the Comanches. To prevent thefts of his reserve ammunition, he and Giselle had made "medicine" before the assembled warriors and convinced them that any interference with the supply would have fatal results. The illusion of sawing his wife in half had been Lampart's main feature, baffling Chief Ten Bears and his medicine woman completely.

"Maybe the folks are running a bluff, pretending that Simmy and Giselle are still around ready to hand over the ammunition on the day," Belle guessed. "Only Ten Bears is figuring on calling them."

"It could be," Dusty admitted. "One of the parties we saw after we pulled out could have recognized Giselle, told Ten Bears, and he's trying to get her back. Or he may think that she's got the photographs Lampart took of him and the medicine woman."

"They thought he'd captured their souls when he showed them the pictures," Emma confirmed. "But why go back, E- . . . Dusty?"

"Because those folks need me and the boys' guns," the small Texan replied. "Having us there could maybe help them hold out until the army arrives."

"I'll ride with you," Belle offered without a moment's hesitation. "You'll be able to use another gun."

"We could use a battery of Williams rapid-fire cannon," Dusty replied. "But I'm not taking you along, Belle. Mark'd have my hide if I did and we all got killed."

"Leave me to deal with Mark Counter," Belle suggested, smiling a little at the small Texan's somewhat peculiar excuse. "Even if we all do get wiped out by the *Kweharehnuh.*"

"I wouldn't want to put ole Mark to any trouble," Dusty replied. "Anyways, I need you to deliver the money to Governor Howard for me."

"Her?" Emma snorted, suspicion right out in the open as she spoke the single, challenging word.

"Why not '*her*'?" Belle challenged.

"I can just see Belle Starr delivering close to half a million dollars to Governor Howard," the blonde scoffed.

"Are you saying I wouldn't?" Belle hissed, fists clenching.

"With a price on your head—" Emma began in a milder tone, realizing that the time was anything but right for an open, head-on clash with the lady outlaw.

"There's no warrant out for me in Texas," Belle declared. "Or any other place, comes to that."

"Innocence, Belle?" Dusty grinned.

"Lack of proof." The lady outlaw smiled back.

"I know she'd do it for me, if she gives her word to," Dusty told Emma. "And you don't need to worry. Before I pull out, I'll give you girls your cut. Then you're free to go wherever you choose."

"Even if I say that I want to go back to Hell with you?" Emma asked.

6

HE'LL BE BACK,
WITH COMPANY

"Was I a suspicious man, which nobody could right truthfully say I am," announced the Ysabel Kid, holding his rangy, mean-looking blue roan gelding to a steady but mile-devouring walk, "I'd be asking myself just what did make those two gals conclude to come back to Hell with us."

"I've been thinking long on that myself," Waco drawled, keeping his black and white *tobiano* mount alongside the Kid's blue roan. "And anybody's likes can say *I'm* a suspicious man; as long as they do it polite and not twice on the same Sunday."

"Trouble being, you've got no pride." The Kid grinned. "Anyways, what's all this-here thinking got you?"

"Not a whole heap," the blond youngster admitted. "Was it just Emma, I'd say she's going and hoping Dusty'll take her to church 'n' make a honest woman of her when we get back."

"Emma's smart enough to know it'll be more *if* than *when*

we get back," the Kid pointed out. "Likewise, she's smart enough to know there's no chance of Dusty doing it."

"They do tell me all women're a mite foolish and a whole heap hopeful when it comes to getting took to church and being made honest," Waco answered. "Could be Giselle's going back to hear the will read, her being a widow-lady and all."

"She's a widow, for sure, you saw to that," growled the Kid. "But I wouldn't lay no 'lady' brand on her."

"You mean she's a *man?*" Waco demanded with carefully assumed interest.

"I don't know and I'm not caring," the Kid replied. "Was you wanting to find out, sneak off and look next time she goes. They do tell that women're different from us."

"How, pappy?"

"They squat, 'stead of standing when they only want to pee—or so I've allus heard tell."

"Now why's they do that, would you say?" Waco wanted to know.

"You should've asked Red last night," drawled the Kid. "Likely she could've told you. I for sure don't know."

Despite their casually cheerful discussion, the Kid and Waco never relaxed in their ceaseless vigilance. Always their eyes searched the surrounding terrain and they carried their rifles instead of leaving them in the saddlebag. With the sun sinking toward the western horizon, they had already covered almost thirty miles of the journey back to Hell. That put them on the fringes of the *Kweharehnuh*'s stamping grounds and, if the Kid's theory about Giselle Lampart should prove correct, moving deeper into danger with every sequence of their mounts' hoofbeats. A quarter of a mile behind, Dusty Fog escorted the two subjects of his companions' conversation.

The small Texan had not agreed to permit the women to accompany him without some argument, discussion, and heart-searching. Nor was he yet convinced that he had acted for the best in concurring with Emma's and Giselle's demands to come along.

After the Kid had returned the previous night and said that the *Kweharehnuh* would be unlikely to come back, Dusty had organized things in a brisk, businesslike manner that had won Lieutenant Kitson's approval. In fact, there had been moments when the young officer had found himself on the point of snapping into a brace and answering "Sir" as Dusty had rattled out some command or instruction. By the time the bodies had been buried and the camp generally settled down, Kitson had been convinced that Dusty was telling him the truth and was willing to carry out his request for further assistance.

Taking advantage of the soldiers accompanying the Kid to search for the rest of their stampeded horses, Dusty had talked with the women. Although Red and the other saloon girl had not argued when they had been told they would each receive twenty thousand dollars—the increased amount having been granted as there was a smaller number to take shares—Giselle had sulked and pouted in her disappointment. She had been expecting a far greater sum than the fifty thousand dollars given to her and was inclined to be rebellious until Emma had intervened. Drawing the brunette aside, the blonde had talked quietly but earnestly to her. At first Giselle had been in vehement disagreement with Emma's proposals, but had finally and grudgingly yielded to them. Much to Dusty's surprise, the blonde had then suggested that she and Giselle should return to Hell with the three Texans.

Dusty's first instinct had been to refuse, for he had not underestimated the dangers of going back. Slowly but surely, Emma had won her point and was granted permission. She had repeated her statement that Dusty, the Kid, and Waco would not be popular with the citizens of Hell and had suggested that her presence and that of Giselle might be in the trio's favor. On hearing why, Dusty had been compelled to admit that the blonde was making sense.

Before giving his permission, however, the small Texan had insisted on learning the real reason for the request. As he had suspected, Emma had financial rather than humanitarian motives. There was a fortune in jewelry in Hell and she hoped to lay hands upon some of it. Sufficient, in fact, to make up for the reduction in the sums she and Giselle had been forced to accept as their share of the mayor's ill-gotten gains. To prevent a similar happening, Emma had extracted Dusty's promise that any loot she and Giselle gathered would be their property and not handed over to the authorities.

Even with that much knowledge, Dusty might have refused; but Emma had pointed out that she might still have been able to ruin the good impression he had made on Kitson. There had also been the point of keeping Belle's true identity a secret for Dusty to consider. Emma had hinted that she would tell the officer the truth and dispel his belief —due to carefully planted hints—that the lady outlaw was the Rebel Spy. There had been a heated scene between Belle and Emma, which Dusty had ended by agreeing to the blonde's suggestion.

Belle had once more requested to accompany Dusty's party, although on less mercenary grounds than those of the blonde. Not only had Dusty refused, but he had obtained her agreement to deliver the money for him. Neither the Kid nor Waco had been surprised by the trust Dusty placed in the lady outlaw. Apart from her close relationship with Mark Counter,[1] Belle had a strong sense of personal honor. Once she had given her word to carry out a project, she would do so without hesitation. The three Texans had been certain that when—or, as the Kid had said, *if*—they came back from Hell, they would learn that Belle had carried out her part in the assignment.

By the time the men had returned, everything had been settled. Each woman had collected her cut of the money and concealed it. Although Red and the other saloon girl had

1. How that relationship began, developed, and finally ended is told in the "The Bounty on Belle Starr's Scalp" episode of *Troubled Range, The Bad Bunch, Rangeland Hercules*, the "A Lady Known as Belle" episode of *The Hard Riders*, and *Guns in the Night*.

asked if they could ride with Dusty's party, they had been persuaded to accompany Belle and the soldiers. Kitson had shown no hesitation about escorting Belle and the two girls to Wichita Falls and acting as custodian of the wagon's load until such time as "the Rebel Spy" could hand it over to Governor Howard. If he had been surprised by Dusty saying that Emma and Giselle would not be going with the other women, he had hidden it very well. That could have been due to the women's stories. While the blonde and brunette had insisted that they were going to their original destination, the girls had declared that they only wanted to reach civilization as quickly as possible.

So everything had been arranged. Waco and Red had spent the night together and had parted at dawn without too great regrets. Knowing that nothing could come of their association, the girl had accepted that it had been enjoyable and profitable but was now at an end. Red was to put her windfall to good use, returning to her home town, marrying well, and settling down to a life of happiness and respectability. For his part, it would be a few more years before Waco met the girl who persuaded him to settle down in matrimony.[2]

No fool, Kitson had noticed certain inconsistencies in the story he had been told. The signs of physical strife on the lady outlaw's and Emma's faces, taken with the money being in the wagon that the saloon workers had obviously been using, had pointed to the whole party traveling as a single unit. However, he had been willing to accept that the blonde and her companions had helped Dusty and "the Rebel Spy" to complete their assignment and asked no embarrassing questions. He had agreed to deliver a message to the governor, requesting that the army should move into the Palo Duro as soon as possible. Without mentioning the town, Dusty had given an accurate description of its location and asked that the soldiers be sent there.

Dusty, the Kid, Waco, Emma, Giselle, and Belle had all

2. Told in: *The Drifters.*

offered up silent prayers that the army would receive the news and reach the town in time to save it being wiped out by the *Kweharehnuh*.

Dawn had seen the two parties going their separate ways. After swinging to the north until hidden from Kitson's view, to keep from adding to any suspicions he might have been harboring, Dusty and his companions had turned to the southwest. By using the riding technique known as "posting the trot,"[3] they had made good time through the day. It had not been easy on the women, but, fortunately, both had done considerable riding in Hell and were fired by their eagerness to reach the safety of the town. "Safety" would be a relative name for it, but at least they would have the buildings in which to shelter if they should be attacked by the Indians.

Unless, of course, the enraged citizens of Hell shot them on sight.

Their reception would depend upon the reaction to the story concocted by Emma and Dusty. If it was accepted, they might be spared by the citizens and would only need to worry about the *Kweharehnuhs'* retaliation when it became obvious that no ammunition was forthcoming.

Bearing in mind the possibility that Giselle might have been the target of the *Kweharehnuhs'* attack on the camp, Dusty had insisted upon taking precautions against ambush. The Kid and Waco had spent their time ranging ahead or on the flanks of the women's line of march. Although there had been no sign of human life all day, the Texans did not regret having taken such preventive measures.

"What do you reckon those folks'll do when they see us riding in, Lon?" Waco inquired, becoming more serious.

"I'd say *if* they see us, it all depends on what *we* let 'em do," the Kid replied. "Or do you figure on Dusty taking us a-whooping and a-hollering, 'Look, folks, we're back!' along the main street comes high noon?"

"I'll let you go in front if he does," Waco promised. "It's a

3. Described in detail in: *Under the Stars and Bars.*

pity you don't have your ole nigger hoss along. He'd surely
look elegant a-heading the parade."

Due to the necessity for avoiding the drawing of attention
to similarities between their real identities and those of the
Caxton brothers and Alvin "Comanche" Blood, the trio had
not been able to use their favorite horses on the assignment.
The big paint studs often ridden by Dusty and Waco bore,
respectively, the brands of the OD Connected and Clay Allison's CA ranches.

Although it had never been branded, the Kid's magnificent white stallion was too large and distinctive to be overlooked. By leaving it in the care of the OD Connected's
horse wrangler—one of the few people who could handle it
in comparative safety—divesting himself of his usual all-
black clothing, and refraining from demonstrating too much
of his prowess with the Winchester or his bowie knife, the
Kid had contrived to prevent the citizens and outlaws in Hell
from suspecting whom he might be.

While speaking, Waco and the Kid had been climbing a
ridge. They did not permit conversation to override caution.
Instead of continuing over the rim, they halted below the
skyline. Elevating their heads, they peered at what lay on the
other side.

"Now there's a feller who's just asking to get hisself
scalped," the Kid remarked.

Following the direction of his companion's gaze, Waco
was inclined to agree with the cryptic comment. About a
quarter of a mile away, a man was riding across their front.
Holding his big blue-black horse to an ambling walk, he tra-
versed the bush-scattered terrain as if he did not have a care
in the world. Tall, well built, with darkish hair, the man wore
the dress and rig of a cowhand. He had on a low-crowned,
wide-brimmed Stetson hat, red shirt, dark blue Levi's jeans
that looked new and hung outside his high-heeled, spur-
decorated brown boots. A brown gun belt about his middle
carried an ivory-handled Colt Cavalry Peacemaker in a contoured, fast-draw holster on his right thigh. For all his appearance, he did not sit his range saddle like a cowhand. He

was leading a well-ladened pack horse at the end of a long line.

"Could be he's an owlhoot looking for Hell," Waco suggested.

"Ways things are right now," the Kid drawled, "he's likely to find it a whole lot sooner than he'd figured on. Only it won't be the 'Hell' he's hunting."

"That's for sure!" Waco breathed, swinging his gaze from the rider. "You see 'em, Lon?"

"Ten minutes back," the Kid exaggerated, and twisted in his saddle to wave for Dusty to keep the women away.

Even when he became aware of the half a dozen *Kweharehnuh* braves who had appeared and sat watching him, the rider displayed no great alarm. Instead, he merely lifted his right hand in a friendly greeting. His behavior indicated that Waco had guessed correctly about his station in life. If he was an outlaw on his way to Hell and under the impression that he had nothing to fear from the *Kweharehnuh,* he received a rapid and unmistakable disillusionment. Instead of responding with an amiable gesture, one of the younger members of the Comanche group raised and fired a Spencer carbine.

As the bullet hissed by his head, the man gave a startled jerk and let go of the pack horse's lead rope. He did not, however, take the appropriate and sensible course of trying to gallop to safety. Instead, he tilted to the left and his right hand wrapped around the wrist of a Winchester rifle's butt. Sliding the rifle from its boot, he straightened up on the saddle. Two more of the *tuivitsis*—there was only one warrior of *tehnap* status present—cut loose with their repeaters. Neither hit the man, but one's bullet spiked up an eruption of dirt to his horse's right. The other's lead rose in a vicious whining ricochet that passed within inches of the animal's right ear.

Giving his first hint that he had realized conditions had changed in the Palo Duro, the man attempted to rein around his mount. At that moment it was rearing its forelegs into the air and trying to back away on the hind limbs. It was moving to the left and its rider attempted to guide it in the opposite direction. His unequally distributed weight caused the horse's hind legs to slide to the left and its front hooves thrust forward in an unavailing bid to regain its equilibrium.

Despite his casual disregard for what the watching Texans regarded as essential precautions of Palo Duro life, the man proved himself capable of swift movement in an emergency. Almost before his mount's right rump had hit the ground, he had freed his feet from the stirrup irons and kicked his left leg forward across the animal's neck. Springing clear, he landed on slightly bent legs and the Winchester rifle's wooden foregrip slapped into his left palm.

Fast though the man had reacted, he had not done so a moment too soon. Letting out ringing war whoops, the braves jumped their mounts from stationary to a gallop almost in one motion. They fanned out, boiling down the slope at reckless speed and each with the same intention: to be the one who counted coup on the hated white brother and who, by doing so, would be entitled to the first pick at the victim's property.

Taking the brass butt of the Winchester to his shoulder, the man sighted and fired at the nearest of the warriors. Down went the *tuivitsi*'s horse, head shot and buckling forward as its legs folded beneath it. With typical Comanche agility, the young brave not only quit the stricken animal's back and landed without injury, but he hit the ground running. Without a moment's hesitation after his narrow escape, he continued to bound onward.

"We'd best go lend the feller a hand," the Kid commented as the attack was launched, signaling with his heels for the blue roan to start moving.

"Be best," Waco confirmed, and his *tobiano* sprang forward alongside the dark Texan's mount.

Topping the rim, the Kid and Waco unshipped from their saddles. They released the split-ended reins, ground-hitching the horses as effectively as if they had knotted the leather straps to a saloon's hitching rail. Advancing a few strides, so that the noise of their shots would not be too close to the horses, the Texans prepared to help the stranger.

While his horse struggled to its feet and loped away until stopped by its trailing reins, the man turned his rifle on the dismounted Indian. He himself was under fire from the rest of the braves, but he did not allow that to fluster him. Taking aim as the brave bounded onto a rock, he fired. Hit in the head, the *tuivitsi* threw aside his Winchester carbine and pitched over backward. Lead hissed around the man, but none of it struck him. None of the *tuivitsis* had had sufficient experience to perform accurate shooting from the back of a war pony thundering at top speed over sloping, irregular ground.

Maybe the *tehnap* in the party would have had better success, but fate—in the shape of the Ysabel Kid—robbed him of the opportunity. Having decided that the experienced warrior posed the greatest threat to the man, the Kid had nullified it with his "old yellowboy"[4] rifle. Standing erect, the dark Texan lined and fired with what barely seemed time to take aim. For all that, the *tehnap*'s head snapped back sharply and he slid rearward over his mount's rump.

Delaying only long enough to kneel and support his left elbow on his bent right knee, Waco blasted the *tuivitsi* who had started the shooting from his fast-moving bay pony.

Ignoring their companions, the remaining trio of *tuivitsi* kept shooting and advancing. Knowing that there was no other way to save the white man, the Kid turned his rifle on the center rider. Through the swirl of powder smoke, he saw that he had made a hit; but the man had also selected that particular *tuivitsi* as his target. Waco's rifle had sent the right-hand warrior sliding sideways from his horse, but the last of the attackers was drawing closer. He was rapidly approaching a distance from which he would be unlikely to miss, even from a moving base.

The sound of hooves from behind reached the Kid's ears.

4. "Old yellowboy": name given to the brass-framed Winchester Model of 1866.

More than one horse at that. Not that he felt alarmed, guessing correctly that Dusty had come up to lend a hand. Either with the small Texan's permission, or disobeying orders, the women had followed him. Emma and Giselle came over the rim just after the Kid and Waco fired their second shots.

Eager as he might be to count coup, the *tuivitsi* knew enough to watch more than his intended victim. He had detected the two ride-plenties on the other slope and noticed a third coming to join them. Then his eyes went to the women. Instantly all thought of killing and loot departed from his mind. There was something of greater importance on hand, a matter which could not even be delayed while he shot down the unhorsed white man.

"White witch!" the brave yelled, whirling his mount into a tight turn that saved his life.

Three bullets, any of which would have struck a vital region of his person, went by the *tuivitsi*'s body as he made the abrupt, violent change of direction. Guiding the pony in a weaving line, he flattened himself along its neck to offer a smaller, more elusive target. It said much for his early training that he escaped with his life. Four times the Kid's rifle cracked, but the flying lead narrowly missed its mark. Then the *tuivitsi* had rocketed over the rim and was gone from sight.

"Ole *Ka-Dih*'s"[5] siding with the *Kweharehnuh,* not the *Pehnane,* today," Waco commented, having watched the Kid's abortive attempts to hit the departing *tuivitsi.*

"Could be we'll come to regret it," the dark-faced Texan replied grimly. "He saw Giselle, yelled 'White witch,' and took off like the devil after a yearling. Likely he'll be back, with company."

"Which case, I'll go catch that feller's hoss," Waco drawled. "This'll not be a good place to be when him and his company get here."

While the young blonde went to gather up the man's mount and pack horse, Dusty, the Kid, and the two women

5. *Ka-Dih:* the Great Spirit of the Comanches.

rode down the slope. Resting the barrel of his rifle on the top of his shoulder, the man turned toward them. His eyes narrowed a little as they flickered from Emma to Giselle and back. However, he advanced with a friendly smile on his lips.

"I reckon I owe you gentlemen my thanks," the man said. "My name's O'Day. My friends call me Break."

7

THEY WANT HER FOR SOMETHING

Dusty Fog matched Waco's summation concerning Break O'Day's presence in their vicinity. So, without being too obvious about it, he studied every detail of the man's appearance.

First item of interest, the gun belt was the rig of a fast man with a Colt. If O'Day could use it to its full potential, he would be a man to be reckoned with in a corpse-and-cartridge affair. Of good quality, his clothes and boots showed signs of hard traveling, but they were otherwise newly purchased.

Turning his attention to O'Day's face, Dusty found it more interesting than his clothing or armament and rig. Good looking, tanned, it had an almost unnatural smoothness. Either he had shaved recently, or had a very slow beard, for his cheeks, top lip, and chin were devoid of hair. His eyes looked strangely sunken for such a fresh, healthy face and their brows seemed almost artificially bristly. Deep brown in color, the eyes were cold, yet strangely compelling in the intensity of their scrutiny. His voice had a slight, educated East Coast accent. It came out with a clarity that suggested it had been trained for being heard distinctly at a fair distance.

Having caught both O'Day's horses without any difficulty, Waco rejoined his companions. Dusty's quick examination of the animals told him that they were good stock, selected for their respective duties. Although somewhat older than the man's clothing, both riding and pack saddles had cost good money and were fairly new. From the look of it, the coiled rope strapped to the saddle horn had never been used.

"We'd best get moving, Mr. O'Day," Dusty suggested. "That buck's likely gone to fetch help."

"The way he was coming for me, I didn't think he'd need it," O'Day replied cheerfully. "I don't know what he shouted to you, but it sounded like one hell—if the ladies will pardon the term—of a mean cuss word."

"You could say that," the small Texan drawled, seeing no point in enlightening the man as to what the brave had said. "Let's move. Maybe you'd best stick with us for a spell, mister."

"I'll be obliged for the opportunity of company," the man declared. "Unless my presence will discommode the ladies."

"If that means do we mind having you along, the answer's no," Emma put in, her eyes raking O'Day from head to toe in just as thorough but more noticeable scrutiny than Dusty had given the man. "Say. Haven't I met you somewhere?"

"I would hardly have forgotten so charming and beautiful a lady as yourself, ma'am," O'Day replied, with a flourishing bow, and turned to take his reins from Waco. "My thanks to you, young feller."

"Twarn't nothing," Waco drawled. "You-all wanting for me to take a point, Brother Ed?"

"Go to it," the small Texan replied, pleased that the youngster had not forgotten to revert to using their assumed names. "And don't you ride with your eyes closed, boy."

"I only do that when I'm asleep." Waco grinned. "Look after my big brother, Miss Emma."

The blonde made no reply, but sat her horse and continued to stare at O'Day with puzzled, suspicious wariness.

"This'll be your first trip to Hell, Mr. O'Day?" Emma inquired, after the man had mounted and the party started moving.

"Does my destination show so plainly?" the man countered.

"I'd say 'yes' to that, way you took on when those *Kweharehnuh* bucks showed," the Kid put in. "Way you waved and all, you acted like they was your rich old uncles."

"If I only had some," O'Day sighed, then nodded to Emma. "But you're right enough, dear lady. I'm going to Hell for health reasons. A hanging always makes me feel ill, especially when it's to be my own. But my remark might shock you and your delightful companion."

Although O'Day had aimed part of his speech in her direction, Giselle did not respond. Yet, like Emma, she had been paying a great deal of attention to the man's appearance, actions, and words. A puzzled, almost nervous expression played across the little brunette's face. Seeing the man's eyes turning toward her, she deliberately swung her head away. It was left to Emma to answer O'Day's politely put comment.

"Neither of us've been shocked since we found out for the first time that boys have things that girls don't," the blonde assured him. "And there's a lot of folks in Hell feel like you do about hangings."

"You know of Hell?" O'Day inquired.

"We live there," Emma replied. "Happen you're so minded, you can ride along with us, Mr. . . ."

"O'Day, but I hope that you will all call me Break. It's a foolish name, but my father was something of a wit. He used to call himself 'End.' "

"That should have been a whole barrelful of laughs," Emma said dryly.

"You'd best go help Brother Matt, Comanch'," Dusty suggested.

"Yo!" assented the Kid, and set the blue roan to traveling

at a faster gait toward where Waco was riding ahead of the others.

"I was assured that the Indians could be trusted up this way," O'Day commented as the Kid took his departure.

"They can, most times," Dusty answered. "Up closer to town, anyways."

"Where the lookouts can see them?"

"Uh-huh. I thought you'd not been to Hell before."

"I haven't. But my informant was pretty thorough," O'Day answered, and looked at Dusty in a calculating manner. "You may remember him. Dipper Dixon. One of Joey Pinter's gang."

"I can't recall any such name," Dusty stated.

"He wasn't in your class, Mr. Caxton," O'Day praised. "You are Ed Caxton, aren't you?"

"So they tell me," Dusty admitted. "But I don't mind this Dixon *hombre.*"

"He was a nothing," O'Day sniffed. "All he did was tell me about Hell and that you'd killed Joey Pinter."

"Pinter had notions along that way about me," Dusty explained. "He died of a case of slow. Are his boys on the way back?"

"I shouldn't think so. They told me that Hell's an expensive town and none of them struck me as having enough brains to pull off a worthwhile robbery," O'Day replied, then he turned his gaze to Emma. "Is there something wrong with me, Miss . . . ?"

"Name's Emma Nene," the blonde introduced. "I don't know what it is, but there's something about you seems mighty familiar."

"I've heard it said that everybody reminds somebody else of an old friend," O'Day commented. "Perhaps I look like a friend from your past?"

"No, you don't *look* like anybody I've ever known," Emma declared. "Who does he remind you of, Giselle?"

"N-nobody!" the brunette answered, still avoiding meeting O'Day's eyes.

"Nobody, dear lady?" the man inquired, a faint hint of

mockery in his soft and polite tone. "I thought perhaps that I might recall some long-forgotten memory. A lover perhaps . . . ?"

"N-no!" Giselle exclaimed, and there was fear on her face. "I—I'm a married woman."

"Your husband is to be congratulated," O'Day told her. "But I'm crushed. I felt sure that I must remind you of somebody. Oh, well. I must be wrong. Surely you ladies can't be going to Hell?"

"We live there, both of us," Emma replied. "I own the saloon and Giselle's husband's the mayor."

"Then I could hardly be riding into town in better company," O'Day answered, "with you as my escort—"

"D- . . . Ed!" Emma interrupted. "Look at Comanche and Matt!"

The two young Texans had turned their horses and were galloping back. Seeing that he had caught the others' attention, the Kid pointed toward their left. Swinging their gaze in the required direction, the women, Dusty, and O'Day received a shock. Some twenty or more *Kweharehnuh* warriors sat their horses on a ridge slightly over a quarter of a mile away.

"Whee doggie!" Dusty breathed, and hefted his Winchester carbine so that the Indians could see it. "Show them your rifle, mister."

"Shoot?" O'Day inquired as he did as Dusty had said.

"Just show them we've got repeaters, first off," Dusty corrected him.

"Now what?" Emma demanded with surprising calm.

"'Less we're lucky," Dusty answered, "some of us are about to get killed."

"Let's fight!" O'Day demanded.

"Only if they force us to it," Dusty replied. "We'll make a run for it. If that pack horse won't come along, turn it loose."

"All I own in the world's on it!" O'Day protested.

"It'll not be a little mite of use to you after you're dead and scalped," Emma pointed out. "Say when you want us to run, D- . . . Ed."

"Leave us hear what ole Comanch' says first," Dusty advised. "Emma-gal, keep us between you and the Indians."

"You can count on me for *that!*" the blonde declared.

"Well?" Dusty said as the Kid and Waco brought their horses to a rump-sliding halt. "What's their play now, L- . . . Comanch'?"

"I'm damned if I know," the Kid admitted, knowing that the tension must really be hitting at Dusty for him almost to make a slip in the use of the name. "I thought I knew all about Comanches, but this-here's got me licked to hell and back the long way."

"How do you mean?" O'Day inquired, fingering his rifle nervously.

"It's what them bunch up there's doing," the Kid answered.

"But they're not doing *anything!*" O'Day pointed out.

"*That's* what's worrying me," the Kid told him soberly. "They've just been a-sitting and a-watching up there when they should've come down and at us so fast we'd've thought the hawgs'd jumped us."

"Perhaps our having Winchesters scared them," O'Day suggested. "They'll have learned what repeaters can do, I'd say."

"Should have, mister," Waco drawled, watching the braves with undeviating attention, "seeing's now how every last mother's son of 'em's toting either a Henry, Winchester, or Spencer."

"Know what I reckon, Ed?" asked the Kid, indicating the interest that the braves were displaying in one member of his party.

"Do tell," Dusty requested.

"They're not fixing to jump us right now. Nor so long as it looks like we're taking Giselle back to Hell."

"Could be, Comanch'. There's that *tuivitsi* who got away from us. He recognized her and that's him sitting next to the war-bonnet chief."

"Shows a man could allus learn given the right teacher."

The Kid grinned, "You couldn't see that good when we first joined up together."

"Why thank you 'most to death," Dusty growled. "Now tell me something that's going to help us out of this tight spot."

"Keep your trust in the Lord, brother," the Kid obliged, raising his gaze piously in the manner of a hellfire-and-damnation circuit-riding preacher. "If he'd be willing to look favorable on a bunch of miserable sinners like us." Red-hazel eyes swung toward O'Day, who was displaying growing alarm. "Leaving you out, friend. Happen you're not a miserable sinner like the rest of us."

"Right now I'm wishing that I'd led a better, cleaner life," the man answered. "I want to go to the town of Hell, not the other one."

"Given time, you'll likely make both of 'em," the Kid remarked. "Only not right now."

"Why not, Lon?" Waco asked, and could have cheerfully bitten off his tongue after his mistake on the last word.

" 'Less I miss my guess," the Kid drawled, and swung from his saddle, "those boys aren't looking for no war. They just want to see Giselle safe to home."

"Why are they so interested in the lady's well-being?" O'Day wanted to know. "Charming and gracious as she undoubtedly is, I'm sure that the Indians wouldn't appreciate her sterling qualities."

"They want her for something or other," the Kid answered, carefully easing a piece of his property from the folds of his bedroll. "Question being, what'd it be they want her for?"

"Could go up and ask 'em," Waco suggested, having identified the item in the dark Texan's hand.

"Happen I'd've figured *that* out in an hour or two," drawled the Kid. "But, seeing's how you licked me to it, I lose and'll have to be the one who does it."

"You allus was a good loser, Comanch'," Waco praised.

"That's just another name for a dad-blasted fool," answered the Kid.

With that, the Kid opened out the item. It proved to be a buckskin cylinder with a heavy fringe on its lower edge and covered with decorative symbols colored red, white, and blue. Sliding his Winchester into the mouth of the tube, he vaulted afork his saddle and looked at Dusty.

"Happen they're not in a talking mood, head out toward Hell. 'Bout a mile on, there's a buffalo wallow you can fort up in—if you can reach it."

"What's that on Mr. Blood's rifle?" O'Day inquired as the Kid rode slowly toward the *Kweharehnuh*.

"It's the medicine boot of a *Pehnane* Comanche Dog Soldier," Dusty explained. "It's kind of a lodge symbol, like a wapiti's tooth is to the Elks. Boot the rifles."

"Boot the rifles!" O'Day yelped. "You mean put them away?"

"Do like Brother Ed says, *hombre*," Waco ordered, as he obeyed. "White folk aren't Injuns. They don't hold guns at a peace treaty meeting."

"You mean—?" O'Day began, but did not comply with Dusty's demand.

"Matt means that Comanch's asking for a parlay and we've got to do things right if he's got 'yes' for an answer," Dusty elaborated, thrusting his carbine into its boot. "So put up that Winchester."

"You mean to trust a bunch of savages?" O'Day growled.

"We can't whip them in a fight, or run fast enough to escape—especially with that important pack horse of yours along," Dusty drawled. "So trusting them makes good sense to me. And I'm getting quite sick of seeing that rifle in your fist. Boot it, *pronto*."

Any soldier who had served in the Texas Light Cavalry's hard-riding, harder-fighting Company C during the war, or cowhand who had worked for the OD Connected, would have identified Dusty's tone of voice instantly. Gentle, almost caressing, it carried more menace and determination than a whole range of bellowed, blustering orders.

Suddenly, to O'Day's amazement, the small Texan was no more. He had been replaced with what appeared to be a man who towered over the others by the sheer driving force of his personality. There had been no suggestion of bombast or open threat in the quietly spoken words, just an assurance that the speaker intended to be obeyed.

"You're calling the play, Mr. Caxton," O'Day stated, and leaned over to replace his rifle in its boot. Straightening up, he managed a smile and went on, "But if you're wrong and I get killed, I'll never forgive you."

Halting a hundred yards from his companions, the Kid set about preparing the way for what he hoped would be a peaceful parlay. Cradling the rifle encased in the medicine boot on the crook of his left arm, he held his bent right arm in front of his chest with his palm open and downward. By moving the raised arm from left to right with a wriggling motion, he announced that he, too, was a member of the *Nemenuh.*

At some time in the distant past, a party of the People had been making a long journey in search of fresh hunting grounds. There had been disagreement among the travelers as to which was the best course, to advance or return to the territory they had left. Those who wished to turn back had done so and the others had referred to them as resembling a snake going into reverse along its tracks. Since then, a Comanche—no matter to which band he belonged—always used the sign of "the snake going backward" when he wished to declare the identity of his tribe to other Indians.

Having stated his connections with the *Nemenuh,* the Kid continued to signal other information. Taking hold of the medicine boot at the wrist of the rifle's butt and muzzle, he raised it above his head so that the *Kweharehnuh* could identify its symbols. After raising and lowering the rifle three times, he removed his right hand and turned the butt forward with the barrel gripped in his left fist.

As clearly as if the Kid had shouted the words in his most fluent Comanche, the braves—or the *tehnaps* and the chief, for sure—had received his message.

"I am *Nemenuh.* A *Pehnane* Dog Soldier, and I want to talk in peace."

"Looks like they aim to make talk," Waco breathed, as the chief answered the Kid's signal and the dark Texan started the blue roan moving up the slope. "I came close to being scared they wouldn't."

"I didn't come close," O'Day commented. "I *was* scared."

Flickering a grin at the man, Waco noticed something so out of the ordinary that it intrigued him. The evening sun was still warm and O'Day was clearly feeling the strain of their situation as much as, or even more than, Dusty and the blond youngster. At least they had the advantage of knowing that the Kid had been reasonably confident of success. Yet the man's face showed none of the sweat that dappled both Texans' features.

In later years, Waco would gain considerable acclaim as a very shrewd peace officer and, by his ability to observe and reason things out, be able to solve a number of puzzling crimes.[1] Even with deadly danger hovering so close, the youngster could still take an interest in the unusual. So O'Day's absence of perspiration was a source of speculation. Either the man was a whole heap cooler and less worried than he was acting, or he could control whatever internal function caused sweat to roll. Waco wondered which, or what other unforeseen circumstance, was responsible for the phenomenon.

Although satisfied that the danger of an immediate attack was over, Dusty did not allow himself to become complacent or incautious. So he turned to study the terrain behind them. As he had expected, the two women were holding weapons. Emma had taken out the nickel-plated, pearl-handled 1851 Model Navy Colt that had been thrust into the waistband of her divided skirt. Gripping a compact, equally fancy Colt 1871 House Pistol with a four-shot "cloverleaf" cylinder, which she had carried in the pocket of her riding jacket, Giselle was pointing the .41-caliber-muzzle of its one-and-a-half-inch barrel at the center of O'Day's back.

1. Told in: *Sagebrush Sleuth, Arizona Ranger, Waco Rides In,* and *Hound Dog Man.*

"Watch where you're pointing that gun, ma'am," Dusty advised quickly, but gently.

Giselle's thumb was resting on the little revolver's hammer. If she drew it back, the unguarded trigger would emerge from its sheath ready to be pressed and make the weapon fire. Being aware of how light that particular model of Colt could be on the trigger, Dusty had felt that a warning was called for. At his words, the brunette snatched the revolver out of alignment. Her face showed guilt that appeared to go far beyond that caused by having been caught in a stupidly dangerous but inadvertent act.

"I have never felt happy around ladies who hold guns," O'Day commented, swinging around. "So few of them take precautions with one in their dainty hands, I've always found."

"Who are—?" Giselle began, in a strangled, frightened tone.

"Lon's coming back—Brother Ed," Waco said, and the brunette's question went unfinished.

"It's all right, Ed," drawled the Kid, riding up. "They'll not bother us—just as long as we keep going toward Hell."

"Why are they so friendly?" O'Day asked. "The ones we met earlier weren't."

"They was just a bunch of *tuivitsis,* young bucks, wanting to show what ornery, mean cusses they were," the Kid replied. "Seems like Doc Connolly, Happy Youseman, and some of the others allowed that there'll be an ammunition handout same as always, Ed. Only Ten Bears'd heard about Giselle pulling out and didn't believe it. So he sent the braves to fetch her back. Now she's headed that way, they allow it's all right and we can go on."

"May I ask why Giselle—if a chance-met stranger may be permitted to make use of your given name, ma'am—is so important to the allocation of the ammunition?" O'Day said, looking at Dusty.

"She used to help her husband trick the Comanches so they wouldn't try to steal *our* ammunition," Emma explained, for the brunette refused to answer.

"Now I see," O'Day stated. "You must be the lady who is sawn in half. Your husband must be a very competent illusionist, Mrs. Lampart."

"He w—" Giselle commenced.

"A real good one, friend," Dusty put in, before the brunette could announce her widowhood. "They'll not fuss any with us, huh, Comanch'?"

"Not so long as we're taking Giselle back," the Kid confirmed. "Seems ole Ten Bears wants to see the whole ceremony when the ammunition's handed over."

"But they can't!" Giselle croaked, realizing what was meant. "Nobody can work the sawing-in-half routine. I'm going back—"

"You try it and we're all dead," warned the Kid. "Ma'am, your only hope of staying alive is to make for Hell."

"That's what we'll do," Dusty declared. "Once we're there, Giselle, we'll figure out some way of bluffing him. Find us a place to camp, Comanch'."

"Keep riding awhiles, there's a stream up ahead," the Kid replied. "Have somebody on guard all night. You won't get attacked, but some of the *tuivitsi* might try their hand at raiding."

"That's hoss stealing to us civilized white folks, mister," Waco informed O'Day. "Way you talk, Comanch', anybody'd think you wouldn't be along with us."

"They'd think right," drawled the Kid. "I won't. Wolf Runner, the chief up there, allows that I've got to ride with him and his boys. Just so's he can be sure the rest of you'll keep going to Hell."

8
I DON'T WANT TO
GO TO HELL

"Suppose we tell ole Wolf Runner we're right took with your company?" Waco demanded, scowling at the Comanches on the rim. "And that he can go climb up his own butt end."

"He wouldn't like that one li'l bit, boy," the Kid replied. "And, seeing's how all the cards're stacked his way, we don't have a heap of choice but play 'em how he wants it."

"We could show him that we mean business," O'Day suggested.

"He'd right soon show *us* that *he* means it even bigger," drawled the Kid.

"The odds wouldn't be much greater than against that bunch that attacked me," O'Day pointed out. "And they didn't impress me as being smart or dangerous warriors."

"You'd've likely learned different if we hadn't happened along," the Kid warned quietly. "See, they wasn't but *tuivit-sis;* which same's young hotheads who don't know better'n charge in head down and horns a-hooking blind. Those fellers up there though, they're most of 'em *tehnaps*. Old, sea-soned-on-red-meat bravehearts, with hair hanging on their belts. Mister, even with us having happened along, you'd find them both smart and dangerous."

"So you conclude to do like Wolf Runner wants, Co-manch'?" Dusty asked.

"He done the concluding for me," the Kid corrected. "Only, just so long's you get Giselle back to Hell right-side-up and with all her buttons fastened, everything'll be fine. No ten-coup war leader's going to let hurt come to Long Walker's grandson, unless he can offer a real good reason for doing it."

"You ride careful, mind, you blasted Comanche," Dusty ordered, with more concern than command in his tone. "Is there anything you'll be needing?"

"Nary a thing." The Kid grinned. "Fact being, I'll likely be living better'n you white folks. Us Comanches know how to travel well-fed and comfortable."

Although Dusty and Waco had serious misgivings, they raised no further objections to their *amigo* being held as a hostage. They had faith in his superior knowledge concerning the risks he was taking. All they could do would be to ensure that they carried out their side of the agreement.

"I don't want to go to Hell!" Giselle whined as the Kid rode back to join the waiting *Kweharehnuh*.

"Nobody does, but they go on sinning just the same," Waco replied. "And, even without Comanch' being held hos-tage, you'd get there, one or other of 'em, whichever way you headed."

"We've no other choice but go on, Giselle," Emma went on firmly. "Don't fret yourself. Ed'll see that nothing bad happens to you."

Although Giselle looked anything but convinced, she kept quiet and accompanied the rest of her party in the direction of the stream. If O'Day's behavior was anything to go by, he shared with the brunette in feeling ill at ease. He constantly twisted in his saddle, searching the surrounding terrain with wary and worried glances. After a short time, however, he relaxed. All of the Indians had disappeared, taking the Kid with them, and the man could detect no sign of them. Neither could Dusty nor Waco. Their examination of the locality was less obvious, but possibly more thorough than O'Day's. The apparent dearth of watchers did not fool them. They both knew that keen-eyed wolf scouts were keeping them under observation all the time.

In passing, Dusty nodded toward the buffalo wallow the Kid had mentioned as a place in which they might have been able to fort up and fight. It was about a hundred yards from the stream, a large depression worn by countless bison rolling on, pawing at, and generally churning up the ground.

"That's where we'll bed down for the night. In the bottom. It won't be comfortable, but no raider can sneak in on us down here."

"How about wood for a fire?" O'Day asked, looking around. "We'll have to carry it from the trees by the stream."

"*You* can go fetch some, if you're so minded," Waco drawled. "But me, I sure don't aim to chance it."

"I thought that the Indians had given us a safe passage to Hell," O'Day pointed out.

"They have," Dusty agreed. "Only they don't trust us a whole heap and're having us watched."

"Where?" O'Day gasped, swiveling around and glaring about him. "I don't see anybody!"

"They're wolf scouts, trained to follow, watch, and not be seen," Dusty explained. "It's work for *tuivitsis,* not *tehnaps.* Happen one of them should see you all alone in the woods, he might not be able to resist the temptation to count himself an easy coup."

"They stop resisting *real* easy, friend," Waco added. "There's never enough coups to go 'round for all the young bucks who want 'em."

By that time, the party had reached the edge of the stream. Dismounting, they removed the horses' bits and allowed them to drink. Giselle kept darting glances from O'Day to the range across which they had been traveling.

She took her mount—one of the dead soldier's horses, borrowed by Dusty from Lieutenant Kitson—a short way downstream of the others. Tired from the exertions of the day, Emma felt little desire to make conversation and paid no attention to the brunette. O'Day resumed his investigations into the habits of the Comanche, so Dusty and Waco did not notice Giselle's furtive actions.

"What is this 'counting coup'?" the man inquired. "Is it another name for taking a scalp?"

"Nope," Dusty replied. "It rates as more important than that, to the Comanches, anyways. They say that anybody can scalp a dead man, it proves nothing. But to count coup shows that the feller doing it has courage."

"But how—?"

"The brave has to touch his enemy, either while killing him or soon after, and say, '*A:he!*', which means 'I claim it.' Once that's been done and said, he's counted coup."

"Way ole Comanch' tells it," Waco went on, "there ain't nothing sets up a lusty young buck like plenty of loot and to've said '*A:he*' good and often. And the Comanches don't go for no taking seconds, thirds, nor fourths."

"That went right by me," O'Day admitted.

"Some of the tribes let the second, third, and fourth braves to touch an enemy count lesser shares in the coup," Dusty elaborated.

"They do say Osages let 'most anybody who wants to share the coup, whether they was around to touch the body or not." Waco grinned. "Could be they just don't like Osages."

"The Comanches figure that they've got so many enemies, they don't need to share coups," Dusty drawled. "All the other tribes called them the *Tshaoh*, the Enemy People, and most times, that's what they used to be."

"You gentlemen appear to know a lot about Indians," O'Day praised.

"All we know, Comanch' taught us," Dusty answered. "His mother was the daughter of a *Pehnane* Comanche war lodge's chief. Which's just about as high as a man can get in the tribe."

"I thought your friend was a half—" O'Day began, then, as frowns came to the Texans' brows, revised his words. "Part Indian."

"He's all white to *us*, mister!" Waco growled.

"No offense intended and I hope none's been taken," O'Day apologized and, with the air of wanting to change the subject, continued, "Is a brave's statement that he has counted coup always accepted?"

"If there's any doubt on it and he's challenged, the band's medicine man or woman can have him swear to it on the sacred sun oath," Dusty answered. "No Comanche will dare to lie after he's taken it."

"Do their medicine people have that much of a hold on them?"

"Their religion has, anyways. They take their beliefs a damned sight more serious than most white folks take God."

"But they must believe in magic if Simm- . . . Giselle's husband could take a hold of them with tricks."

"Only if it's some kind of trick they've never seen and don't know how to pull," Dusty corrected. "Their medicine men and women have been pulling things out of the air and the like since afore Columbus landed. No, sir, don't sell Simmy Lampart short. I didn't see him do it, but that sawing-his-wife-in-half trick must've been something special to fool the *Kweharehnuhs'* medicine woman."

Something had been said that Waco instinctively knew had significance beyond the general trend of the conversation. He scowled and tried to recall just what it had been. Before he could do so, an interruption came that drove it temporarily out of his thoughts.

While the men had been talking, Giselle had allowed her mount to drink and had then led it away from the water. Emma was kneeling on the edge of the stream and bathing her face. Nobody was looking at the small brunette as she turned the animal's head to the southeast and swung into the saddle. If she had given more thought to her actions, she might have met with greater success in her desertion. Instead of walking slowly away, she gave her mount's ribs a sharp kick, which made it grunt and bound forward.

"What the—?" Waco spat out, spinning around with hands fanning to the butts of his Army Colts.

Also alerted by the sudden thunder of hooves, Dusty and O'Day turned with equal speed. They, too, sent their hands toward weapons. Crossing his body, Dusty's palms enfolded the grips of his Peacemakers. All in a single, incredibly swift blur of movement, the matched Colts left their holsters and the hammers clicked to full cock. Although O'Day matched the small Texan's speed in turning, his long-barreled revolver had not cleared leather by the time Dusty was standing ready to shoot.

Shuffling hurriedly on her knees, Emma clawed to free the Navy Colt from her waistband. Anger flickered across her face as she saw, not an attacking *Kweharehnuh* warrior, but Giselle Lampart galloping away as fast as the borrowed horse would carry her.

"Stop the crazy bitch!" Emma screeched, furious at the thought of Giselle—who was vital to her plans for enrichment—behaving in such a stupid manner.

That proved to be a piece of needless advice. Waco reacted to the desertion without the need for prompting. Twirling the Colts on his trigger fingers, he caused them to return to their holsters with the minimum of effort on his part. Then he caught hold of the *tobiano's* saddle horn and swung himself onto its back. Reaching forward, he jerked free and drew back the hackamore that was fixed to the bridle's *bosal*.

The horse Waco sat belonged to his work mount[1] when back at the ranch, and it had been trained with careful patience. So it responded to his command of "Back," despite the lack of bit and reins to augment the single word. Instantly it started to retreat from the water's edge; chin tucked

1. Texas cowhands used the word "mount," not "string," for their work horses.

in, neck well flexed, hind legs moving in long, confident strides, and forefeet taking deliberate steps. Waco sat with relaxed, easy balance, his vertebrae perpendicular for greater control of his horse's movements.

Once clear of the water, the blonde struck the *tobiano*'s near shoulder with his right spur. At the signal, its forelegs left the ground and it pivoted fast on its rear hooves. With its head pointing after the departing brunette, it was urged into motion. Like the *tuivitsis* earlier, the youngster built his mount's pace up to a gallop in a very short time. Doing all he knew how to increase the speed, he guided it across the range.

"Shall we go after them?" O'Day asked, allowing his weapon to slide back into its holster.

"Likely Brother Matt can handle it," Dusty answered, and returned his guns to their holsters. "What the hell's gotten into Giselle, Emma?"

"She's scared that the Indians will want her to be sawn in half when they come for their ammunition," the blonde guessed, glaring after the riders and stabbing the Navy Colt into her waistband. "With Simmy dead, there'll be nobody who can handle the trick."

"You say that Si- . . . her husband is dead?" O'Day put in harshly.

"He was shot by some of my people when they robbed him," Emma explained, using the excuse she had arranged to make on her arrival in Hell. "We're just on our way back after hunting them down."

"Look there!" Dusty gritted, pointing toward the wooded land that fringed much of the stream's banks.

Having no wish to let the conversation continue on the subject of Mayor Lampart's death, the small Texan had been seeking a way to end it. Providence had presented him with the means to do so. Looking in the direction he was pointing, Emma and O'Day let out exclamations of surprise and alarm. A stocky young Antelope brave stood on the edge of the trees, his repeater cradled on his left elbow and his whole attitude showing that he was watching the pursuit of Giselle.

"Like I said," Dusty drawled. "Wolf Runner's got us watched."

"How long has he been there?" Emma breathed, hand creeping toward her revolver and voice showing tension.

"All the time," Dusty answered.

"What shall we do?" O'Day demanded.

"Nothing we can do, except wait for Brother Matt to fetch her back safe and sound."

"And if he doesn't?"

"Mister," Dusty said quietly, "*if* he doesn't, we're in with the water over the willows and a fast stream running."

"Huh?" O'Day grunted.

"It's what trail drivers say when they're in just about as bad trouble as they can find," Dusty explained.

"You've been on trail drives then?" O'Day asked.

"Some," Dusty admitted, wondering if apprehension over their danger or some other reason had prompted the question. "You'll likely see what I meant, happen Matt doesn't bring her back."

"So will Comanche, even worse than we do," Emma put in bitterly. "That stupid, no-account little tail-peddler.[2] She's got cow droppings for brains. Damn it all, without her—"

The blonde stopped speaking, realizing that she had come close to saying too much about her plans and reasons for having persuaded Giselle to accompany her in the return to Hell.

"She's scared of something," Dusty answered. "Well, we'd best make out that we figure everything's all right. Let's take the horses back to the buffalo wallow and start making camp."

"Your *brother* hasn't caught her yet," O'Day commented, peering across the range and laying emphasis on the second word. "But I'm sure he will. You are a remarkably competent family."

At first, Giselle maintained her lead on Waco. That did not surprise the youngster, as he had already analyzed the

2. Tail-peddler: a prostitute, especially one of the cheaper kind.

situation and formed correct conclusions based upon his practical knowledge of equestrian matters. Smaller and lighter than her pursuer, Giselle possessed no other advantages in her flight. She was neither such a good rider nor so well-mounted. Kept short of cash by a Congress more concerned with winning votes than expending the taxpayers' money on defense projects, the United States' Cavalry could not afford to purchase high-quality mounts for its enlisted men. On the other hand, Waco sat a horse belonging to a ranch that selected only the best for its riders and insisted that the animals be kept in the peak of condition.

So Waco realized that, barring accidents, it was inevitable he must overtake her.

On they raced through the gathering twilight—not an ideal time to be riding at a gallop over unfamiliar terrain. For all that, the woman encouraged her mount to greater efforts with cries, jabbing heels, and slapping reins. Apart from an occasional soft word of praise, Waco rode in silence and concentrated on what he was doing. Controlling his speeding *tobiano*'s natural inclination to increase its speed until it was rocketing along blindly, he watched Giselle for any hint that she had become aware of his presence to her rear.

None came. What did show were growing symptoms that the brunette was rapidly losing control over her horse. By that stage of the flight, however, it was getting blown and its pace was starting to flag.

Nearer thundered Waco, edging the *tobiano* to the brunette's left. That had been done deliberately. It was unlikely that Giselle would show sufficient good sense to halt, so he intended to give her no choice in the matter. Having been trained in the typical white man's fashion, the cavalry horse had always had its rider climb on or off at the near side. If it felt its burden leaving over the right flank, its reactions might be unpredictable and dangerous to her or Waco.

Coming level with the woman, the youngster saw her head swing in his direction. Even as she opened her mouth to either speak or scream, at the same time attempting to rein her horse away, he leaned across and coiled his right arm

about her waist. Giving her no time to resist, he cued the
tobiano with knee pressure so that it veered away from the
other animal. In her anxiety, Giselle had inadvertently
helped Waco. The cavalry horse had shown little response to
her manipulation of the reins, but it angled off slightly and
furthered the blonde's efforts at removing her from the saddle.

Giselle screeched, a mixture of fear and anger, as she felt
herself being dragged sideways. Luckily for them both, she
had sufficient understanding of the position to kick her feet
free from the stirrup irons—but she did not release her grasp
on the reins.

Alarmed by the unexpected disturbance of the weight on
its saddle, the cavalry horse started to shy even farther to the
right. Giselle's rump and right leg slid across the seat until
she was clear of it and hung suspended from Waco's encir-
cling arm. Fright more than sense caused her to release the
reins, but they had already snatched the horse's head
around. Disrupted by the woman's actions, its head drawn
abruptly in a new direction, the animal lost its footing. It
went down and rolled over. Fortunately, the *tobiano* had
turned just far enough to the left and galloped by without
adding to the cavalry horse's troubles by trampling upon it.

Using what guidance he could exert with the hackamore,[3]
Waco set about bringing the *tobiano* to a halt. Still screech-
ing, Giselle tried to reach his face with her fingernails. Spitting out a threat to drop her, he slackened his hold a little.
That brought an end to her attempts to scratch her way free.
Waco steered his horse in a wide curve, which ate away its
galloping momentum. On reaching a walking pace, he lowered the kicking, still protesting brunette to the ground.
Then he rode to where her horse had regained its feet. Dropping from his saddle, he allowed the *tobiano*'s hackamore to
dangle free and walked up to Giselle's mount. Although

3. The use of a hackamore and *bosal* is described in detail in: *A Horse
Called Mogollon* and in *.44 Caliber Man.*

badly shaken by the fall, heavily lathered, and winded, it did not appear to be seriously injured.

Pattering footfalls came to the youngster's ears as he straightened up from examining the horse. Turning, he found a wild-faced Giselle bearing down furiously on him. Spitting out what he took to be obscenities in some foreign language, the brunette thrust her right hand into its jacket pocket. Seeing the Colt House Pistol emerging, he did not hesitate. For all that, she had moved with such speed that he was almost too late. Leaping toward the little woman, he watched the snub-nosed revolver come clear of the pocket and line in his direction. Its hammer went back under the pressure of her thumb, causing the trigger to click out its sheath to where her forefinger was waiting to press it.

Around lashed Waco's left hand. He struck Giselle's extended right wrist and deflected the House Pistol's muzzle. Flame spiked from the short tube and the bullet it propelled could not have missed the youngster by more than an inch. The narrow escape brought an instant reaction. Even before the incident, he had never liked Giselle's ways or morals. So he was less inclined to take her sex into consideration than he would have been with most women. Letting out a low, savage hiss, he drove his right hand in a slap that sent her spinning around and away from him. Dropping the House Pistol, she tumbled facedown and lay sobbing, with both hands clutching at her cheek.

"Get up!" Waco ordered, retrieving the House Pistol and tucking it into his jeans' pocket.

Something in the youngster's tone caused Giselle to obey. Crawling to her feet, she turned a tear-stained face in what she hoped would be a pleading and pathetic manner to him.

"D-don't take me b-back there!" Giselle pleaded. "I—I'll share my money with y-you."

"Like hell," Waco replied. "You start walking back where we come from. And, lady, if Lon gets killed through this, I'll do just the same to you."

9
MEPHISTO'S BEEN DEAD
FOR YEARS

"This'll do us," Dusty Fog declared, drawing rein and nodding to where a spring bubbled up through the floor of the valley the party was crossing. "We'll make camp while there's still light to put on Scotch hobbles."

"You're using them again?" O'Day inquired. "They're hell to take off."

"That's why we're doing it," Waco drawled, throwing a pointed glance at the sullen, drooping Giselle Lampart as she sat her horse at Emma Nene's side.

"She won't run away again," the blonde promised grimly.

"I thought you said we aren't far from Hell," O'Day remarked, as the Texans and women dismounted.

"It's maybe five miles from here," Dusty answered. "Happen you're that way inclined, Break, you can ride on and find it."

"In the dark?" the man queried, glancing significantly to

where the sun was sinking below the western rim of the valley.

"Should be able to *hear* what you can't see, you go on a ways," Waco drawled. "Hell comes alive after dark and sounds like Trail Street in Mulrooney when the drives are in."

"Despite of which, you are staying here until morning," O'Day pointed out. "That means you have a very good reason, Ed."

"Good enough," Dusty confirmed as he loosened the girths and worked his saddle back and forward to cool the horse's back. "What with Simmy Lampart being dead, the ammunition supply destroyed, and the *Kweharehnuh* acting sort of restless, there'll be guards out around town. They'll be jumpy and won't shout, 'Halt, who goes there, friend or foe?' until *after* they've thrown lead at whoever's coming to make sure they can't do anything but halt."

"Even if they can't shoot good, they could get lucky," Waco supplemented, scowling at Giselle as if wishing that he could send her to try out the sentries' skill or luck.

It was sundown on the day after Giselle's attempted flight. Unencumbered by the wagon, Dusty and his companions had been able to travel faster than on the escape from Hell. So his estimation of the distance separating them from their destination was fairly accurate.

The day's journey had passed uneventfully, yet not without anxieties for Dusty and Waco. There had been no sign of the *Kweharehnuh* scouting party who were holding the Ysabel Kid as a hostage against Giselle's return to Hell. Shortly after the brunette had ridden away, a second wolf scout had joined the first. They had talked, clearly discussing the situation, and the second *tuivitsi* had departed—presumably to take the news to Wolf Runner. Having waited until Waco returned with Giselle, the first wolf scout had faded off. Since then, the small Texan and the young blonde had been consumed with fears for the Kid's safety.

To take their thoughts from their *amigo*'s possible fate, Dusty and Waco had kept up a conversation with O'Day for much of the day's journey. On their side, they had tried to discover more about the mysterious man who had been thrown into their lives. O'Day had answered asked—and unasked—questions frankly and cheerfully. From what he had told them, he qualified for entrance to Hell and he had cleared up the matter of Eastern manners and Western appearance to their satisfaction. When Waco had pointed out that he could not have purchased such a well-designed gun belt at short notice, O'Day had laughingly reminded them that it was possible to purchase such an item in the civilized and peaceful East, provided one knew where to look and what to ask for.

For his part, O'Day had expressed a lively interest in all matters pertaining to the Comanches in general and Antelope band in particular. Although his questions had commenced on general topics, he had worked them around to the subject of the powers of the medicine men and women. He had also been eager to hear how Lampart had won—or tricked—his way into the *Kweharehnuhs'* confidence and had obtained permission to build Hell in their domain.

Any details that the Texans had been unable to supply had come from Emma. It was the blonde who had told O'Day of another precaution Lampart had taken to protect his interests against the Indians. In addition to having convinced them that sudden death would come to any man who tried to steal his ammunition or molest legitimate visitors to the town, the mayor had had photographs taken of Ten Bears and the medicine woman. Believing that he had captured their souls, the spiritual and material heads of the band had been more amenable to his will and disinclined to make trouble for him.

No matter how amiable and pleasant O'Day had tried to be, Giselle had refused to have anything to do with him. She had lost some of the fear that had tinted her expression when being addressed by him the previous night but made it plain that she wanted only to be left alone. After a succession of direct snubs and monosyllabic answers, O'Day had accepted defeat and concentrated his attention on Emma and the Texans. Dusty had noticed several times that Giselle was willing to observe O'Day, even if she refused to speak to him. Stealing surreptitious looks at the man, the brunette's face had shown mingled emotions. Interest, curiosity, alarm, and disbelief played on her features, which would be swiftly turned aside if the object of her scrutiny looked at her.

Having sound reasons for wanting to arrive unnoticed in Hell and knowing that—as a result of precautions against accidental discovery taken by Lampart—the town came to life at night, Dusty had had no intention of making his entrance before dawn. Nor had he wished to let O'Day go in to spread the news of their coming. To prevent arousing the man's suspicions when he discovered how close to town they had halted, the small Texan had produced a valid and acceptable excuse for delaying their appearance until daylight.

"In which case, having as great an antipathy toward being shot as I felt regarding my being hung, I will bow to you gentlemen's superior wisdom," O'Day declared cheerfully. Swinging down from his saddle, he went on, "If the ladies can bear the proximity of my presence for another night, I will be honored to spend it in their company."

"I can never resist anybody who calls me a lady." Emma smiled. "Feel free to stay on with us, Break."

"When you've off-saddled, Emma, you and Mrs. Lampart might's well go to the other side of the spring and pick the best bedding spots out," Dusty suggested. "We'll tend to the horses."

Obtaining the added security offered by Scotch hobbling, as opposed to using the conventional leather cuffs and linking swivel chain of double hobbles, was a time-consuming business. There was some need for haste as the sun, dipping below the rim of the western slope, threw dark shadows over the spring. Removing their saddles and leaving behind the ropes from the horns, Emma and Giselle carried out Dusty's instructions. They hauled their rigs around to the western edge of the water hole, out of earshot of the men.

Making a large loop with Giselle's rope, Waco draped it around the cavalry horse's neck and tied a bowline knot behind the near shoulder. Then he took the longer end of the rope over and made a half hitch about the right hind leg just above the ankle joint. Carrying the end of the rope forward and up, he secured it to the loop in such a manner that the trapped limb was raised and its hoof suspended about four inches above the ground. Held in that manner, the horse could neither stray far nor move at speed. In addition, as O'Day had commented, removing the Scotch hobble was not easy—especially when attempted in darkness and with the need to avoid making any undue noise.

While Dusty did not believe that Giselle would try to escape again, he had no intention of presenting her with the opportunity. If he had been able to hear the conversation taking place between the two women, he would have felt less certain about the brunette's acceptance of the situation.

"Do you have your pushknife on you, Emma?" Giselle inquired with what she hoped sounded like casual interest, setting down her saddle.

"No!" the blonde answered, and frowned at the brunette. "If I did, I wouldn't let you have it."

"I only wanted to—"

"I know what you want to do with it and the answer's still 'no.' Hell, Ed won't let the folks do anything about us leaving them the way we did."

"He's not your 'Ed Caxton,' " Giselle spat out. "He's Dusty Fog!"

"Hold your voice down, damn you, or you'll be muttering through bloody gums!" the blonde hissed furiously. "If O'Day hears—"

"All right, don't get mean!" the brunette whined, knowing that Emma's temper could be explosive on occasion.

"Anyways, seeing that he is Dusty Fog, you should be even more sure that he'll look after you. A feller like 'Ed Caxton' might have said the hell with you and let the folks do what they want. Dusty won't."

"It's not what the people will do that bothers me. Or having to do the trick. We both know you can handle Simmy's part easily enough as long as the box hasn't been damaged."

"Then what is it?" Emma demanded.

"Who does that feller O'Day put you in mind of?"

"Nobody that I can remember. His face isn't familiar."

"Not the face," Giselle corrected. "His voice."

"His voice . . . ?" the blonde repeated. "Yes, it does sound kind of familiar."

"He talks just like Mephisto used to," Giselle said, dropping her tone almost to a whisper and throwing a frightened glance in O'Day's direction.

"Mephisto!" Emma gasped, and for a moment, she looked nearly as frightened as the little brunette. Then she mastered her emotions and gave a shrug. "Aw, go on. Mephisto's been dead for years."

"We don't know that for sure!" Giselle pointed out. "His body was never found and—"

"Take a hold of yourself, you little fool!" the blonde interrupted in a savage manner. "There were a dozen or more people saw him rush out of the hotel and jump into the East River—"

"But his body wasn't found!" the brunette protested.

"If it had've been, you and Simmy would most likely have wound up in jail," Emma said coldly. "That feller's not Mephisto. After what you pair did, his face wouldn't look like that."

"D-don't . . . !"

"And don't you come the harmless little angel with me. I know you, Giselle Lampart, and know how much that's worth. So O'Day talks a mite pompous, like Mephisto used to. I've heard plenty of fellers, actors, magicians, confidence tricksters, and the like, who did. Hell! Look at his face. It's not had vitriol thrown into it. Or do you think he looks like it might have?"

"N-no, it doesn't," Giselle admitted with a shudder. "Emma, I didn't thr—"

"I don't care who threw it!" the blonde snapped. "Mephisto's dead. Only your guilty conscience makes you think O'Day is him. So forget any fool notions of running away again. We've too much at stake to have you hurt."

"Yes, *we* have," the brunette agreed, and her fears appeared to flicker away. "And I'm the only one of *us* who can open the locks and safe doors."

"Don't get smart, little half sister," Emma warned. "If you double-cross me, I'll show you that I can be as mean as Mephisto would be if he was still alive and caught up with you."

"D-don't even think things like that, Emma!" Giselle pleaded.

Seeing the men approaching, the women allowed their conversation to lapse. Darkness had come down by the time Dusty, Waco, and O'Day had spread their bedrolls and the women had made ready for the night.

"I could drink a whole gallon of coffee," Emma remarked, looking at Dusty.

"Why not light a fire and make some?" asked a familiar voice, drifting from the blackness of the western slope.

At the first word, the blonde let out a startled yelp, which mingled with Giselle's squeal of alarm. Instinctively Dusty, Waco, and O'Day reached for their guns. Only the Easterner completed his draw and even he did not fire. Coming on foot out of the gloomy shadows, the Kid grinned cheerfully at the various signs of alarm caused by his unheralded arrival.

"You folks're sure jumpy," the dark Texan commented, halting with his Winchester's barrel resting on his right shoulder.

"Blasted Injun!" Waco snorted disgustedly, hiding his relief at seeing his *amigo* was unharmed. Letting the Colts sink back into their holsters, he went on, "I was like to blow windows in your fool head, thinking you was some other kind of varmint."

"Could you hit me, that is," countered the Kid. "Howdy, Miss Emma, Mrs. Lampart, friend. See this pair of buzzards didn't manage to get you lost."

"Them *Kweharehnuhs* now, they've got right good sense," Waco declared. "They soon enough give you back to us."

That seemed obvious. The Kid might be afoot, but he was in possession of all of his weapons. His attitude of cheerful ease suggested that he had not escaped and wasn't expecting

to be pursued. Staring through the darkness, Emma sought
for hints that he had arrived in time to overhear her conversation with Giselle. Nothing about his voice or attitude suggested that he might have.

"Wolf Runner figured's how you could use some food,
seeing you didn't cook any last night or this morning," the
Kid drawled. "So he sent me over to fetch you some."

"He's surely generous and free-handed with his giving,"
Waco commented, staring from the Kid's empty left hand to
the rifle-filled right.

"I've got it, and enough wood to make a fire, on a pack
hoss up there," the Kid answered. "Left it on the hoss so I
could sneak down quiet-like, 'case you wasn't saying what a
real nice young feller I be."

"Why'd we talk different about you than other folks?"
Waco wanted to know.

"You're just natural mean, boy. Why'n't you 'n' Ed help
me tote it down?"

"I'll come, if you need me," O'Day offered.

"Might be best if one of us stayed on here," Dusty replied,
throwing a meaning nod toward Giselle.

"I only asked hoping you'd say 'no,' " O'Day answered.

"How're things, Lon?" Dusty inquired as they walked up
the slope.

"Easy enough," the Kid replied. "I thought they might get
rough when that wolf scout come to say Giselle'd lit out.
Then the other brought word that the boy'd fetched her
back."

"I'm damned if I know why I bothered," Waco injected.

"Then tonight Wolf Runner was asking why you'd stopped
instead of going on to bed down in Hell," the Kid continued.
"I 'minded him that you're only *white* folks 'n' likely didn't
know for sure where the town's at. Then it figured to him."

"And he let you-all come back seeing's we're this close,"
Dusty guessed.

"Said I could come—"

"Likely got tired of feeding you," Waco interrupted.

"So's I could tell you I'm fixing to go with him to the

village, so's I can say 'howdy' to Ten Bears for Grandpappy Long Walker," the Kid concluded as if the youngster had never spoken. "And he allowed he'd be right honored to have me along."

"I thought you allus reckoned Comanches don't tell lies?" Waco remarked.

"And they don't," confirmed the Kid.

"Then why don't you say truthful that you had to threaten to bust both his legs and make him herd sheep afore he'd agree to be seen in your company?" the youngster demanded. "That's the only way you'd get *me* to agree to take you anyplace. *And* I wouldn't be right honored about it."

"You know how to handle the blister end of a shovel, boy?" Dusty growled, eyeing the blonde menacingly.

"I can't right and truthful claim I do," Waco admitted proudly.

"Keep flapping your lip and, comes us getting back to home, I'm going to improve your education on them lines," Dusty threatened. "You got something special in mind, Lon?"

"Why sure. I aim to find out just why they was so all-fired set on having Giselle come back."

"You don't reckon it's just to see her dance in that fancy li'l costume and be sawn in half?"

"There's a mite more to it than that, I'd say. The braves aren't saying much, but what I can make out, the medicine woman, *Pohawe,* has been getting hoorahed bad over not knowing how Lampart's tricks was pulled. That's not good for her business."

"Could be she reckons she could work out how it's done was she to see it done again," Waco suggested.

"Or she's maybe counting on the folks not being able to do it, with Lampart dead," Dusty went on. "If they can't, their medicine's gone sour and they can be treated like other palefaces."

"That could be," admitted the Kid. "Anyways, I'll see what I can learn. Say, I'm right pleased you didn't have that O'Day *hombre* come with us."

"I concluded you didn't want him along," Dusty drawled.

"You was right. What do you make of him?"

"I don't know, Lon. He's amiable enough to talk to. Way he tells it, he's bad-wanted in a few places and figured to lay low in Hell for a spell. Says he bought all his gear new afore setting off, so he'd be less noticeable than in city duds. Which's true enough. But I don't know what it is, I'm uneasy having him around."

"Could be you're jealous of him being so clean-shaven," Waco put in.

"Huh?" Dusty grunted, laying a hand on his stubble-coated face.

"Yes, sir," the youngster said, delighted at having noticed something that had slipped the small Texan's notice. "He's either shaved when we wasn't looking, or got a face as bald's a girl's."

"I've known fellers who didn't need to shave, even when full grown," the Kid announced. "Maybe you pair've been too busy to notice, but the folks in Hell're still keeping to that no-fires-in-the-daytime ruling."

"We'd noticed," Dusty assured him. "Are the *Kweharehnuh* still letting folk in and out of town?"

"Sure," the Kid confirmed. "Likely Ten Bears's waiting to see whether he gets his ammunition afore he stops it. Anyways, I'll learn all I can at the camp, then come in and let you know how things stand."

10

THE REST OF THE MONEY'S HIDDEN

Walking along Hell's main street, Emma Nene, Giselle Lampart, Dusty Fog, and Break O'Day went by Doctor Connolly's home and office building toward the front door of the Honest Man saloon. Largest building in the town, the saloon alone had two floors. On the upper's veranda rail was nailed a large wooden sign bearing the name of the establishment, but no painting to illustrate the title as was common in such premises elsewhere.

"How could an artist paint something that doesn't exist?" Emma countered when O'Day mentioned the discrepancy.

It was noon and, apart from themselves, the street was deserted, which did not surprise the women or Dusty. In fact they had been banking on finding such a condition.

During their approach from the tree-lined top of the hollow in which the town had been erected, they had seen no sign of human life. For all appearances, the entire population might have been laid to rest in the large graveyard. A few horses were hitched outside the various adobe *jacales* that sprouted irregularly beyond the business premises flanking the main street, and more occupied the livery barn's corrals. The barn's staff had not been present, so the newcomers had tended to their horses unaided and left the animals in previously untenanted stalls. Having been presented with ownership of the barn for his part in removing the original proprietor, Dusty had the keys to its side rooms in his possession. Unlocking the office, he had allowed the others to leave their saddles and portable property until it could be more suitably cared for.

After the Kid's departure the night before, Dusty had told O'Day the story concocted by Emma and secured the man's offer of assistance if it should be needed. So O'Day accompanied the women and the small Texan, while Waco went off to attend to another matter.

To an unknowing observer, Hell would have looked like any other small, sunbaked range-country town. A mite more prosperous in its appointments than most, maybe, but with nothing to hint at its true nature and purpose. Most of the conventional business and social amenities could be located —with the notable exceptions of a bank, jail, or stagecoach depot. There was neither school nor church, but other small towns also lacked them.

Facing the Honest Man stood the lengthy, well-appointed Youseman's Funeral Parlor, which probably had a sobering effect upon revelers who were all too aware that capture by the law would mean death on a hangman's rope. Beyond the saloon and on the same side was Giselle's home, which also combined with the mayor's office and what had passed for a bank.

On stepping through the batwing doors into the large barroom, Dusty, the women, and O'Day found that they could no longer remain unobserved. Although the majority of the room was unoccupied, the stairs and balcony empty of people, six men and a big, buxom, garishly dressed woman sat around what had been Emma's private table. Startled exclamations burst from them as they looked toward the main entrance. An angry hiss broke from the blonde, for the red-haired, good-looking brothelkeeper Rosie Wilson was sitting in her chair at the head of the table.

Dusty recognized four of the men. Tall, gaunt, miserable of features, Doctor Connolly might have been the under-taker and the big, burly, jovial-looking Emmet 'Happy' Youseman, in his checked suit and diamond stickpin, the town's surgeon. Fat, pompous as when he had attended board meetings in the East, the hotel's owner, Emanuel Goldberg, turned red and spluttered incoherently. His part-ner in many a crooked deal, now acting as jeweler and pawn-broker, Sylvester Crouch, muttered something to the nearer of the two strangers.

Although Dusty did not know the pair, he could guess at what they were. Tall, lean, and wearing low-tied guns, they had a matching wolf-cautious alertness. One had black hair and a walrus moustache that did nothing to conceal a hard, cruel mouth. The other was going bald, needed a shave, and had a patch over his left eye. Dressed cowhand fashion, nei-ther of them struck Dusty as having any legitimate connec-tions with ranching.

"Easy, all of you!" Dusty ordered, as the townsmen made as if to rise.

Soft-spoken the words might have been, but they caused the quartet to halt their intentions. The other two male occu-pants of the table exchanged glances, but made no hostile moves.

"Well well, Emma-gal," Rosie Wilson boomed, swinging to face the blonde. "I never thought to see *you* back here."

"That figures, way you're making free with my place and my stock," Emma replied, indicating the bottles and glasses on the table, then the cigars that the bunch around it—in-cluding the woman—were smoking.

"We didn't think you'd dare be coming back," Crouch insisted, altering his words halfway through.

"I can see that," the blonde snorted, swinging a gaze around the room. "I don't think the floor's been cleaned and washed since I left." She turned cold eyes in Rosie's direction. "You're in my chair, *Mrs*. Wilson."

"There's some might say different," the brothelkeeper answered.

"I had my fill of rolling on the floor and hair-yanking with Belle Starr," Emma warned, right hand resting on the butt of the Navy Colt. "So if you want *my* chair that badly, get up and tell me—with a gun in your hand."

"Who're these bunch?" the one-eyed man demanded, his voice showing that he had done more than his share in making free with Emma's stock.

"The folks we told you about, Alec," Goldberg answered. "Emma Nene, Mrs. Lampart, and Ed Caxton. I don't know their companion."

"I'm just a man they met on the trail," O'Day announced.

"Then bill out of things that're none of your concern," the one-eyed man ordered, and swung cold, challenging eyes to Dusty. "You're the yahoo who gunned down Ben Columbo 'n' Joey Pinter, huh?"

"Seemed like a good thing to do at the time," the small Texan replied. "Who're your friends, Happy?"

"Visitors like yourself, Ed," Youseman answered. "Alec Lovey and Jack Messnick. They came in last night."

"See they pay for their drinks before they go to bed," Dusty ordered. "And they look tired enough to go right now."

"You telling us to get out of here?" Lovey demanded, lurching to his feet.

"What we've got to say's for the Civic Regulators' ears, *hombre*," Dusty replied. "And I figure it'd be easier for you two to go than all of us."

"That's big talk for a small man," Messnick stated, also rising. He had taken less to drink than his companion and looked the more dangerous.

"I can back it, if I have to," Dusty assured him.

"Against all of us here?" Lovey challenged, jerking his left thumb around the table.

"There's not but the two of you'll take cards," Dusty

pointed out. "The rest of them know us—and want to find a few things out."

"So two of us's all," Lovey sneered, listening to the confirmatory mutters that had followed the small Texan's statement. "That still puts the odds in our favor at two to one."

"Only it's more like one to one," commented a voice from the rear of the barroom.

Turning their heads, the party around the table saw Waco standing at the doorway that led to the rear of the building. With his left shoulder leaning on the door's jamb and hands thumb-hooked into his gun belt, he contrived to present an impression of deadly readiness.

"Maybe we'll just try taking those odds," Lovey announced, his one eye glinting dangerously.

"Then you just go to doing it, *hombre,*" Dusty offered.

Less drunk than Lovey, Messnick could read the danger signs better. Like other men before him, the outlaw suddenly became aware of Dusty's personality and forgot about him in mere feet and inches. There stood a *big* and very capable man, full able to hold up his end in a shooting fuss. Taking him on in a fair fight would be fraught with peril.

"Aw hell, Alec," Messnick said in a mild tone. "We're here to have fun, not to make trouble. If these folks want to talk private, we should be gentlemen and leave them do it."

"You mean eat crow to this—?" Lovey blazed.

"I mean let's go and grab some sleep," Messnick interrupted, before some unpardonable insult was made and needed to be accounted for. "Come on. Maybe tonight we'll get lucky just like we did that time in Fort Worth."

"Huh?" grunted Lovey, then his puzzled expression turned into a knowing and sly grin. "Sure. Just like in Fort Worth."

If the words carried any special meaning to the other participants in the scene, they failed to make the fact known. Break O'Day looked from the two outlaws to Dusty Fog and then at Emma. The latter couple were apparently giving all their attention to the townspeople. Disappointment showed briefly on the faces of the brothelkeeper and four members

of the Civic Regulators. However, they made no attempt to
address the outlaws. Lurching away from the table, Lovey
accompanied Messnick across the room in the direction of
the main entrance. O'Day sensed that the quartet at the table had expected a more aggressive response to the small
Texan's challenge.

Walking slowly, the men exchanged quick glances and
nods. Their hands had stolen surreptitiously to the butts of
their holstered weapons. Suddenly they sprang away from
each other, turning and jerking out their weapons. On another occasion, they had employed a similar strategy and
escaped arrest at the hands of three lawmen. Neither expected too much difficulty in dealing with two young cowhands.

Just an instant too late, Lovey and Messnick discovered
that their strategy had failed to take their proposed victims
by surprise. Instead of giving his undivided attention to the
Civic Regulators, that *big* Texan was watching *them*. His
young companion—kid brother, by all accounts—no longer
lounged against the door, but was standing erect and looking
even more ready for trouble.

Knowing that his companion would take "Ed Caxton" as
his target, Messnick devoted attention to handling the
"younger brother." The outlaw was the fastest man Waco
had ever faced. So fast, in fact, that he could have completed
his draw and put a bullet into the youngster before Waco's
lead struck home and prevented him. In fact, under the circumstances, Messnick's gun cracked ahead of Waco's Army
Colt going off.

With his revolver lifting into line, Lovey saw the *big* blond
Texan's hands crossing. The outlaw's last living impression
was of flame erupting from the center of his opponent's
body. Before his mind could register the fact that Dusty had
drawn and fired with both hands, two bullets sped his way.
One passed through his good eye, the second puncturing the
patch over his other eye and driving onward into his head. So
close had the shots been together that they formed into a
single sound. Firing once as he pitched backward, the bullet

ending its flight harmlessly in the front of the bar, Lovey's body crashed through the batwing doors and onto the sidewalk beyond its portals.

Where Messnick set his faith in firing from waist-high and by instinctive alignment, Waco had decided that the range was too great for accuracy by such a method. So the youngster had taken the necessary split second to raise his Colt to shoulder level and use its sights. Messnick missed his only chance of survival. On the heels of his shot, the long-barreled Army Colt barked wickedly. Like Dusty, Waco shot for an instantaneous kill. His bullet centered neatly in the middle of the outlaw's forehead. Dropping his gun, Messnick twirled on his toes almost like a ballet dancer. He sprawled face-down on the floor as his companion passed lifeless through the batwing doors.

"Sit still, gentlemen!" O'Day said, but the Cavalry Peacemaker that came into his hand and slanted toward the table made it more of an order than a polite request.

"That goes double for you, Rosie!" Emma warned, producing her revolver. "You're so big I couldn't miss you."

"Easy there!" Goldberg put in, sounding alarmed. "We didn't know what they planned to do."

That was true as far as it went. While the party at the table had not encouraged the outlaws in their actions, the subject for discussion had been that Messnick and Lovey should accompany a group of Hell citizens in an attempt to locate Emma's party. Having arrived without much money, the pair had been willing to go along. The return of the blonde and her friends had removed the need for the posse, which probably had been the cause of the two men's actions.

"How many *amigos* do they have?" Dusty demanded, holstering his Colts.

"N-none," Goldberg answered. "They came in alone."

"Mister," Dusty growled, adopting the character of Ed Caxton once more. "Happen anybody takes up for them, I'll figure I've been lied to—"

"I assure you that they're not with any other visitors,"

Goldberg declared pompously. "We were surprised to see you back, Emma."

"You mean you figured that Emma, Matt, Comanch', and me'd robbed Simmy's office and lit out?" Dusty challenged, nodding his approval as Waco crossed to check up on Messnick and look along the street.

"That was never suggested," Youseman said, in a tone that implied it had been and believed.

"May I ask where you have been since it happened, Emma?" Connolly put in.

"Hunting for the money Hubert, Belle Starr, and some of my gals stole," the blonde replied, so sincerely that she might have been speaking the truth. "Him and the girls grabbed Giselle while everybody was watching Starr and me tangling in the dueling basin. They made her open the boxes and cleared off with her and the money the gang leaders had left in Simmy's care."

"The hostlers at the barn said you told them to have a wagon ready that morning, Ed," Youseman remarked, almost apologetically.

"Sure I did," Dusty agreed. "Hubert had seen me, saying Emma wanted him to collect some supplies. I knew she used the wagon, so I told them to have it waiting for him."

"How did you know about the robbery?" Goldberg inquired.

"Let's sit down and we'll explain everything," Emma countered, going toward her usual chair.

For a moment Rosie Wilson remained seated. Then she shrugged and rose to select another place. Youseman joined Waco at the front doors and told the men, who had been attracted by the shooting, something of what had happened. Having arranged for the bodies to be taken to his place, the undertaker returned to the table with Waco.

"You can thank Brother Matt here for what's happened," Dusty commenced. "He got to thinking why that explosion might have happened and headed for the barn—"

"I didn't want any of the gang leaders to guess what was up, so I made out's I was running afore the *Kweharehnuh* come, all riled over losing their bullets," Waco interrupted, covering a point that Goldberg might have raised if he had recalled their conversation shortly before the youngster had taken his departure. "When I saw the wagon'd gone, I headed after Brother Matt 'n' Comanch' 'n' told them what I reckoned'd happened."

"We got the whole story out of Belle Starr," Dusty continued. "Hubert'd brought her in to help rob the mayor. That's why she'd started those two fights with Emma—"

"And, like a sucker, I let her!" the blonde put in, sounding convincingly angry. "Still, I paid her back good before she died. Say. It's a pity we couldn't fetch her in for you and Doc, Happy. There was a good bounty on her head."

"Did you catch up with Hubert?" Youseman inquired hurriedly, desirous of changing the subject and wondering if the blonde knew their secret or had only been guessing.

"We got him," Dusty confirmed.

"Where is he?" Goldberg demanded.

"Dead, along with all the bitches who helped him!" Emma spat savagely. "There's wasn't a bounty on them, so it wasn't any use us fetching them back."

"There's fifty thousand dollars here," Dusty went on, tapping the bulging left side of his shirt. "The rest of the money's hidden—"

"It's what?" Youseman growled, and his companions showed their indignation.

"Stashed away safe, friend," Dusty repeated. "We didn't know how you'd act when we came back, although we guessed what you'd have been thinking. So we concluded to make sure we got a hearing."

"It's our money!" Goldberg spluttered.

"What didn't belong to the gang leaders was the Civic Improvement Fund," Dusty corrected. "Which last's no more *yours* than it was Simmy Lampart's."

"That's true enough," Goldberg admitted. "But as a committee appointed to run Hell until a new mayor can be elected—"

"That's one problem you don't have anymore," Dusty interrupted. "Mrs. Lampart's taking over as mayor, with Emma to help her."

"Why should she!" Rosie Wilson yelled, starting to rise.

Emma scooped up the revolver that lay on the table before her and lined it at the bulky brothelkeeper. Looking from the muzzle to the blonde's face, Rosie sank down onto her chair again.

"Ben Columbo, Joey Pinter, the Smith boys, and those two yacks who just got toted out of here're right good answers to *that*, ma'am," Waco drawled. "We sided Mayor Lampart against Basmanov's bunch and we'll stand by his widow."

"Matt's put it as well as I could have," Emma went on, laying down the Colt. "Anything Giselle doesn't already know about the town, me, Ed, or the boys can tell her."

"Well . . ." Connolly began.

"What does exhumation mean, Doc?" Dusty asked quietly.

"Digging up a body for—" the doctor commenced.

"I thought it was something like that," the small Texan admitted. "They do say a whole heap of strange things've come to light through exhumations."

"I've heard tell of graves being found empty when they was opened up," Waco continued. " 'Course, that wouldn't happen in our boot hill, now would it?"

Worried glances passed between Connolly and Youseman. They had once been surgeons, experimenting in longevity. Needing human bodies upon which to work, they had begun by robbing graves. Requiring fresh blood and tissues to further their studies, they had solved their problem by murdering healthy patients. When news of their actions had leaked out, they had escaped on a wagon train of assorted fugitives gathered by Simeon Lampart.

The party's original intention had been to reach Mexico. Circumstances had permitted them to settle in the Palo Duro and make Hell a profitable proposition. Connolly and

Youseman had developed a process for embalming the corpses of outlaws killed in the town. With the aid of Lampart's contacts, the corpses had been taken to legitimate towns and the bounties collected on them.

Connolly and Youseman had believed that their secret was known to only four men. From what they had just heard, Emma, possibly Giselle, and certainly the two Texans were a party to it. The pair were all too aware of what their fate would be if news of their activities should reach the outlaws in town.

"I think that Giselle would be an excellent mayor!" Youseman declared. "And it'll save unpleasantness all 'round if we accept her."

"That's true enough, Happy," Crouch enthused. "I'm for it."

"So am I!" Goldberg hastened to declare.

Glancing around, Dusty held down a grin. After Lampart's body had been discovered, there had clearly been controversy over who should replace him as mayor. Unless Dusty missed his guess, two sets of former business associates were divided on the issue. He was also willing to bet that Goldberg's response, having come so quickly after Crouch's acceptance, stemmed from a desire to ingratiate himself with what would become a powerful faction in the town's affairs.

"What happened when the Indians learned that the ammunition shack had blown up?" the small Texan inquired, keeping his thoughts to himself.

"Ten Bears came to see us the next day," Youseman replied. "We tried to convince him that everything is still all right, but he's given us a warning. Either the next issue's made, or he'll run us out of the Palo Duro."

"How long do we have?" Waco asked.

"They're coming for it tomorrow," Goldberg replied. "It's all right, we can make the issue. A few of us didn't think it was advisable for Lam- . . . Simmy to hold the only supply. So we laid in a stock of our own."

"So everything *is* all right," Emma remarked.

"It is *now*," Rosie Wilson answered, with a malicious grin. "You see, Ten Bears wants the *full* handing-out ceremony. And that means he's expecting to see Giselle do her dance— then get sawn in half."

11
IT IS THEIR RIGHT
TO KILL YOU

Walking through the darkness, accompanied by Wolf Runner, the Kid looked at the large, open square of ground illuminated by four huge fires. Just as he had suspected on receiving an invitation to eat with Chief Ten Bears, the affair was not a small, informal family gathering, but a meeting with all the prominent members of the band.

The Kid had felt a pleasurable sense of nostalgia as he had accompanied Wolf Runner's party into the *Kweharehnuh* village shortly before sundown. Apart from the different medicine symbols on the panels of the conical, buffalo-hide *tipis*—the emphasis being on sketches of pronghorn antelope rather than bison—they might have been those of the *Pehnane* Comanche in whose care he had been raised and educated.

Warring against the nostalgia had been a growing sense of concern for the welfare of his *amigos*. There were aspects of *Nemenuh* life going on all around that had been cause for alarm to a man schooled in the ways of the People.

Women and *naivis,* girls of marriageable age, had gathered
in laughing, chattering groups to make or mend clothing,
repair sections of *tipi* walls, or prepare food. Several of the
groups had been engaged in putting up supplies of jerked
meat and pemmican—traditional rations for warriors, being
nutritious and easily transported when away from the village
on scouting, raiding, or fighting missions. Particularly the latter, when there would be little time to spare in hunting for
fresh food.

There had been other, allied preparations being made, the
Kid had observed. Despite Lampart's gift of repeating rifles
and ammunition, the *Kweharehnuh* warriors clearly had no
intention of allowing themselves to become completely de-
pendent upon his bounty. Under the guidance of *tehnaps,*
tuivitsis had been sharpening the blades of knives and
tomahawks. Two old men and a trio of Mexican boy captives
had sat before a *tipi,* busily fletching arrows to be added to a
large number they had already equipped for use. The Kid
had noticed that the barbed heads would be horizontal, instead of vertical, when fitted to the string of a bow. That
meant they had been intended for use against a creature that
stood erect on its hind legs, so that its rib cage was perpendicular to the ground. Such arrows were not designed to be
discharged at whitetail deer, wapiti, buffalo, or pronghorn
antelope.

Outside another *tipi* a *tehnap* had worked with unwavering
attention. He had been packing pages ripped from a thick,
looted Montgomery-Ward catalog into the saucer-shaped interior of a round shield. Beyond the circle of dwellings, *tuivitsis* and *tuineps*—boys not yet old enough to be classed as
warriors—practiced with weapons, or at riding. They had
been concentrating the latter on handling a bow from horse-
back and toward picking up a dismounted or injured companion at full gallop.

Taken individually, the various activities might have been
harmless. Put together, they suggested that the bravehearts
were planning a foray in strength. It might be launched
against the white settlements beyond the Tule and Palo

Duro country. Or the expedition could be aimed at an objective much closer at hand.

There was only one place in the latter category. The town of Hell.

While the rest of the party had headed for their respective *tipis* or to leave their mounts with the horse herders beyond the camp, Wolf Runner had escorted the Kid to the home of the *paria:vo*—the senior, or "peace" chief of the band. The Texan's presence in the camp had attracted some attention, but none of the people had shown more than a casual interest in him. Certainly they had not displayed open hostility at the sight of a white man in their midst. Ten Bears had been courteous and had offered the visitor hospitality. As the grandson of a famous war leader, and a name warrior in his own right, *Cuchilo* rated a dance in his honor. So the invitation had been made and accepted.

Studying the scene before him, the Kid wondered if maybe he was making a mistake in trusting the *Kweharehnuh*. The faces of the onlookers showed no emotion as he passed through their ranks. Yet he sensed an undercurrent of restlessness that was not entirely caused by the prospect of a celebration. On the surface, however, everything seemed normal. Twelve chiefs and war leaders, all wearing their finest clothes, formed a semicircle around Ten Bears. The woman standing at the right of the *paria:vo* could only be *Pohawe*.

Although Ten Bears was nominally a "peace" chief responsible for the administration of the band's domestic and social affairs rather than being a leader in battle, he gave evidence of his earlier martial prowess. In his right hand, he held a seven-foot-long *bois d'arc* war lance with a spear-pointed, razor-sharp head and a cluster of eagle's feathers at its butt. Only the bravest of the *Nemenuh* carried a lance. Ten Bears, as the Kid knew, was one of the very few warriors to have been permitted the honor of retaining his weapon after his retirement from active, fighting life.

Thickset, though running a little to fat, the *paria:vo* was an impressive figure. There was nothing in his appearance to suggest that he might be a drunken degenerate, sucked into an alliance with the white man by a craving for whiskey. He was a tough old Comanche who had never seen the boundaries of a reservation. In his attire, only the gun belt about his middle, with its holstered Army Colt and sheathed Green River fighting knife, was of paleface origin.

From the *paria:vo,* the Kid turned his eyes to the medicine woman. Tall and slim for a *Nemenuh,* Pohawe had short-cropped curly black hair with the part line, trimmed down the middle, accentuated by vermilion. Her features looked more mulatto or quadroon than Comanche, for all their traditional adornment. Red lines ran above and below her eyelids, crossing at the corners. The insides of her ears were colored bright red, and a red-orange crescent had been carefully marked upon each cheek. Numerous bracelets and necklaces attested to her wealth, as did the rest of her clothing. She wore a soft, pliable, muted-yellow buckskin blouse and skirt, covered with intricate beading designs and carrying luxurious fringes on the elbow-long sleeves and calf-level hem. The joining of the blouse and skirt was concealed beneath a coyote-skin peplum bearing several geometric medallions of silver and trimmed with numerous bead-covered leather thongs. The moccasins on her feet had cost somebody much time and labor, being well-made and intricately decorated with still more beads.

Going closer, the Kid was conscious of the medicine woman's eyes raking him from head to toe. He was bareheaded and had donned a clean shirt and jeans for the occasion. Carrying his Winchester in its boot across his left arm, he had his gun belt buckled on. As a *Nemenuh,* he could—and was expected to—be armed when attending such a function. His saddle, bridle, bedroll, and Stetson had been left in Wolf Runner's *tipi,* as he was classed as the chief's guest.

Pohawe's eyes left the Kid. Following the direction in which they gazed, he saw two *tehnap* in the forefront of the onlookers. They had buffalo-hide robes draped across their shoulders, but underneath wore nothing except their breechclouts and moccasins. Each held a tomahawk and a round shield. More significantly, they had war paint on their faces and torsos.

To the Kid, it seemed as if a message passed between *Pohawe* and the pair of braves, although no words had actually been spoken. However, the social courtesies had to be carried out. He came to a halt and raised his right hand in the palm-forward salute that was also a sign of peace. As a guest, it was his place to speak first—especially in the presence of older, respected members of his host's band.

"Greetings, medicine woman; *Paruwa Semenho,* friend of my grandfather, Long Walker of the Quick Stingers; and chiefs of the *Kweharehnuh,*" the Kid said, in the slow-tongued accent of a *Pehnane.* "I come in peace to your camp."

Apart from the speaker being dressed and armed like a white man, there was nothing unusual in his arrival. Any Comanche warrior could expect to be made welcome in the village of another band. A noted war leader like Long Walker would assume that his only grandson was obliged to pay a courtesy visit to the chief of the *Kweharehnuh* while in the Palo Duro.

"Greetings to you, *Cuchilo,* grandson of my old friend," Ten Bears answered. "You will sit with us and eat?"

"My thanks to you, *paria:vo,*" the Kid assented, adopting the half-mocking, half-respectful tone with which a lusty, active young *tehnap* addressed a person who might rank high in social prominence, but who was—in the warrior's opinion—no longer of great importance.

A grin twisted at Ten Bears' lips as he caught the inflection in the Kid's voice. *Cuchilo* might now live with the white people, but he still thought, spoke, and acted like a Comanche.

"Did you also come in peace when you fought with the blue-coat soldiers against Kills Something and braves from this band?" *Pohawe* demanded, speaking loudly enough for her words to reach the ears of the assembled people.

"I did," the Kid confirmed. "They were my friends and I was riding with them. So I fought."

There would have been no point in the Kid trying to conceal the part he had played during the fighting in which the war leader, Kills Something, had died. The survivors of the affray—which had been a prelude to the floating outfit's assignment in Hell—were certain to have told the story of their defeat. It was inconceivable that they would have omitted to mention the man who had played a major role in their downfall. The Comanche had admiration for a shrewd, brave, and capable fighting man, but nothing except contempt for a liar.

"You say you are *Nemenuh*," *Pohawe* went on, clearly directing her words to the crowd as much as to the Kid. "And yet you helped the soldier-coats to kill our braves."

"I am a man of two people," the Kid countered. "And, as I was riding a war trail with white men, I fought alongside them."

"No man can be loyal to two peoples, *Cuchilo*," *Pohawe* warned.

"Who are *you* loyal to, medicine woman?" the Kid challenged.

From the expression on *Pohawe*'s face, the barb had gone home. The Kid felt that he had scored a point of dubious value. As the daughter of an unimportant, not-too-successful warrior and his mulatto captive-wife, she had risen high in the band's society. There were many who resented her position of influence. So she objected to any drawing of attention to her mixed blood. Even if she had not been the Texan's enemy before, she was now.

"Some of our bravehearts were killed!" *Pohawe* gritted.

"And some of the men I rode with," the Kid reminded her. "They all died with honor and as true warriors."

This time the Kid knew that he had made a telling point. Like all Indians, the Comanches set great store by a man dying well and with honor.

"My son died in that fight, *Cuchilo*," one of the "old man" chiefs remarked. "You had dealt with him as a *tehnap* with a *tuivitsi* earlier."

"I remember him," the Kid admitted, thinking of the young warrior whom he had taught a lesson in manners. "He died well, attacking us, and helped others to escape without hurt."

That was not entirely the truth, the *tuivitsi* having been stupidly reckless before meeting his end. However, it helped an old warrior's grief to hear such words. The Kid had made a friend.

"Those two men, Charging Wapiti and Came With The Thunder, had a brother at the fight," *Pohawe* announced, indicating the pair of warriors to whom she had signaled on the Kid's arrival. "They claim you for his death. It is their right to kill you."

"It is *my* right to die fighting," the Kid pointed out. "I am a *Pehnane* Dog Soldier and I have never gone against my oath to my war lodge. I am sworn to die with a weapon in my hand."

"A fair fight, Ten Bears!" boomed Wolf Runner, who had stood at the Kid's side through the conversation. *"Cuchilo* came here as my guest. If Charging Wapiti and Came With The Thunder want blood, let them come singly."

Going by the low rumble of approval that rose from the onlookers, the war leader's words had their support. A *paria:vo* was always a shrewd politician and, as such, Ten Bears knew better than to fly in the face of public opinion.

"A fair fight it will be," the "peace" chief declared. "What weapons will you use, Charging Wapiti?"

Shrugging off his robe, the taller, heavier of the pair stalked forward. He raised the shield and tomahawk into the air.

"These!"

That was caution, for the brothers had heard of *Cuchilo*'s deadly skill with a rifle.

"I'm sorry for your brother's death, *tehnap,"* the Kid declared, handing his rifle to Wolf Runner. "You have no guns, so neither will I."

With that, the Texan unfastened and removed his shirt. Passing it to the war leader, he untied the pigging thongs holding the tip of his holster to his thigh and unbuckled the gun belt. Sliding out the bowie knife, he let Wolf Runner take the belt. As the Kid was about to move forward, the "old man" chief who had asked for information rose. Advancing, he offered the shield that had been resting on his knees.

"Take this, *Cuchilo*," the chief suggested, ignoring the disapproving scowl that *Pohawe* directed at him.

"My thanks," answered the Kid, conscious that he had been paid a great honor. "May it serve me as well as it always served you."

Made from the shoulder hide of an old bull buffalo, heated and steamed until contracted to the required thickness, then pounded and rubbed with a smooth stone to remove every wrinkle, the shield was about two feet in diameter. The space between the separate layers of hide had been packed tight with feathers, hair, or possibly paper, which would deaden the impact from arrows or blows by other weapons. A pliant buckskin cover had been stretched over the convex outer face and laced into position by thongs that passed through holes around the edges. A dozen or so long, flowing feathers were secured to the rim of the outer sheath, and not merely for decoration. Also affixed were the teeth from a Texas flat-headed grizzly bear, indicating that its owner was a mighty hunter. The painted scalps below them told that he was also a famous warrior.

While the chief was making his loan to the Kid, Came With The Thunder discarded his robe and joined his elder brother. The *tuivitsi* whispered in the *tehnap*'s ear, glancing toward the Texan. At first Charging Wapiti appeared to disagree with what was said, then he nodded and gave some advice. Having done so, the *tehnap* advanced a few strides as if eagerly waiting for the duel to commence.

"I don't want this fight, *Paruwa Semenho,* chiefs, and people of the *Kweharehnuh*," the Kid announced, as the chief returned to his place in the semicircle. "But it has been forced on me and I will do all I can to win."

With that, the Texan slipped his left arm through the two stout rawhide loops fixed to the concave inner side of the shield and drew them to either side of his elbow. Moving his arm a few times, he tested the weight and balance of the shield. He gripped the bowie knife in the fashion of a white man, or a Mexican, with the blade extended ahead of his thumb and forefinger.

Experienced eyes took in the way the concave swoop of the false edge met the convex curve of the cutting surface, exactly in the center of the eleven-and-a-half-inch-long, two-and-a-half-inch-wide clip-pointed blade. That was a fighting knife second to none and its owner handled it like a master.

One question was in every warrior's mind. Would the unfamiliar shield be a liability or an asset to *Cuchilo?*

"You insist on your right, Charging Wapiti?" Ten Bears asked formally.

"We do," the *tehnap* agreed. "While that one lives, our brother cannot rest easily in the Land Of The Good Hunting."

"You hear, *Cuchilo?*" the *paria:vo* inquired.

"I hear, *Paruwa Semenho,*" the Kid answered. "And I say to all who can hear, Ten Bears is not to blame whichever way this fight comes out."

While speaking, the Kid had turned to the chiefs. He saw Ten Bears give a nod of satisfaction and approval. The fight that was to come might be justified under Comanche law, but it was well that there could be no cause for complaint from Long Walker. Maybe the *Pehnane* were eating the white brother's beef on the reservation, but the Dog Soldiers had long since established a reputation for being quick to avenge any insult or injury to other members of their lodge. The Kid had absolved Ten Bears of all blame in the affair.

Swinging to meet the first of his attackers, the Kid saw that they had separated. Charging Wapiti crouched slightly, as if preparing to attack. Loud into the silence that had fallen rang a *Kweharehnuh* scalp-yell. It did not come from the *tehnap*'s lips. Instead, the younger brother sprang forward from the Kid's right side.

Although Came With The Thunder had been supposed to be launching an unsuspected, surprise attack, he had committed an error in tactics. Young and inexperienced, he could not resist the temptation to give his war cry before charging at his enemy.

There was no time for the Kid to gain the feel of the shield. Fortunately it was of the same general size, shape, and weight as those he had been trained to use and with which he had practiced when visiting his grandfather. Pure fighting instinct triggered an almost automatic response to the assault.

Pivoting to meet the charge, the Kid saw the *tuivitsi*'s tomahawk hissing toward his head. Throwing up the shield, he realized that it had gone too high and was too perpendicular to cause the blow to strike at an angle and glance off. There was no time to make alterations—and no need. The sharp cutting edge of the war ax thudded against the center of the shield. Meeting the flint-hard yet resilient cover, it rebounded harmlessly.

Like a flash, the Kid swooped his knife around for a low thrust at Came With The Thunder's body. The *tuivitsi* dropped his shield deftly, deflecting the bowie knife downward and to its user's left. Allowing the bottom edge of the shield to slide along the back of the blade until halted by the outward turn of the guard's recurved quillon, the Kid angled his weapon upward. Doing so locked the shield between the back of the blade and the quillon. Helped by the leverage of the quillon's inward bend against the lower phalanx of his forefinger, the Kid raised the blade and shield.

A sudden reversal of direction drew the bowie knife free when it was level with the *tuivitsi*'s shoulder. Shock twisted momentarily at Came With The Thunder's face as realization of his predicament struck him. Nor, if the exclamations that arose on all sides were anything to go on, had the precariousness of his situation escaped the onlookers' attention.

Down and to the left flashed the bowie knife, its cutting edge tearing a shallow gash across the *tuivitsi*'s exposed chest. Gasping in pain, Came With The Thunder fell back a pace and left himself wide open. Even if doing so would have availed him anything—for the youngster was pledged to kill him and would have continued with the attempts to carry out

the oath—the Kid could not have halted his movements. In-
herited, age-old instincts guided what was practically a sub-
consciously directed reflex action. At the lowest point of its
stroke, the bowie knife altered its course. Coming up, it
raked the false edge—honed as sharp as the cutting surface
itself—to its target. Blood burst from the terrible wound as
the bowie knife laid the *tuivitsi*'s throat open to the bone.

Spinning around, dropping his tomahawk, and allowing
the shield to slip unheeded from his left arm, Came With
The Thunder sprawled facedown on the ground in front of
the chiefs. Even with his blood racing in the savage exulta-
tion of having emerged victorious from a primitive conflict,
the Kid did not growl out the coup claim, *"A:he!"* No Comanche would think of counting coup if circumstances
forced him to strike down another member of the *Nemenuh*.

Having watched his brother tumble, spewing out life's
blood onto the turf underfoot, Charging Wapiti attacked.
There was no warning this time. He moved in silence, but
was not entirely unexpected. The *tuivitsi*'s trick had warned
the Kid what to expect. From delivering his killing stroke,
the Texan whirled to face his second assailant. One glance
told him that he would be meeting a far different, more dangerous antagonist. Instead of duplicating his brother's wild,
announced rush, the *tehnap* glided forward in the manner of
an experienced warrior. He would not allow anger, or over-
confidence, to lure him into rashness.

For a few seconds, the Kid and Charging Wapiti circled
and studied each other. They held their shields before them
at chest level, ready to be raised or lowered as the need
arose. Each carried his assault weapon in the manner suited
to its specialized requirements. While the *tehnap* held his
tomahawk's head upward and out to the right, to be used for
sideways or downward chopping blows, the Kid kept his
knife so that he could aim for the torso with a thrust, cut, or
the savage hacking slash for which the James Black bowie
was perfectly adapted.

Although the *tehnap* was slightly heavier, there would be
little difference in their weights. Any advantage that the Kid

gained from his height and greater reach was to some extent
nullified by the tomahawk's sixteen-inch-long, tapering from
one-and-a-half- to one-inch-diameter shaft.

While watching for the opportunity to attack, Charging
Wapiti made circling motions with his left arm. That set the
feathers fringing his shield rippling and ruffling in a manner calculated to bewilder the Kid's eyes and conceal its
wielder's purpose. For his part, the Kid knew that he could
not hope to match Charging Wapiti's skill in manipulating a
shield. So he contented himself with watching and waiting. If
he hoped to escape with his life, he must fight on the defen-
sive until presented with a chance to change things.

With a yell, the *tehnap* bounded forward. He swung his
shield to the left, striking at the Kid's in the hope of knocking it aside. Just in time, the Texan turned his arm, so that
the shields met face to face instead of his being struck on the
side.

Leaning on the *tehnap,* the Kid tried to keep them close.
In that way, he would be inside the swing of the tomahawk,
but could use the point of his knife. Even as the great blade
drove upward and under the shields, Charging Wapiti sensed
the danger and flung himself away. As he went, he swung his
tomahawk toward the Kid's head. Thwarted in his intentions,
the Texan protected himself. Feathers flew as the Kid's
shield rose and halted the war ax.

Around the two men circled, with Charging Wapiti initiat-
ing further attacks and the Kid defending. Such were each's
speed of reactions and body movements, as well as skill with
the shields, that neither could blood his weapon on the other.
Yet both of them had narrow escapes. Once the Kid mis-
timed a block with his shield. Twisting his body like an eel in
a trap, he carried himself clear of the tomahawk's downward
chop. A few seconds later, having had a side cut parried, the
tehnap found his belly once more in peril from the Kid's
hook upward with the clip-pointed knife. He was saved by a
rapid jump to the rear.

Soon after, with the breath hissing through his parted lips,
the Kid was granted a desperate chance. Also showing signs

of the strain, Charging Wapiti had kept up a continuous yet unavailing attack. Drawing away slightly, the *tehnap* flung himself bodily at the Texan. The shields met face to face with a solid crack. To the *tehnap* and the onlookers, it seemed that the impact had knocked the Kid staggering.

Letting out his scalp-yell, Charging Wapiti followed up his advantage and put all he had into a roundhouse swing aimed at the side of his enemy's neck. The Kid extended his left foot as far to the rear as he could take it, bending his right knee and resting the shield on the ground for added support. That carried him under the arc of the other's blow. Instantly, the Kid struck in the manner of an épée fencer delivering a low lunge. Carried forward by his impetus, the *tehnap* met the bowie knife's point. Charging Wapiti's weight combined with the Kid's thrust to sink the blade hilt deep in his belly. Forcing himself erect, the Kid tore his knife free and the *tehnap* went down.

12
YOU WON'T SHOOT ME, MADAM

Although Emma Nene knew that her stay in the town would be limited, she felt completely at home in the barroom of her saloon. With Dusty Fog and Waco to her right and left, she sat on the chair she had always occupied at her private table. The half a dozen gang leaders currently visiting Hell, together with Crouch, Goldberg, and Connolly, were the blonde's guests. All things considered, the slight air of tension was understandable.

There had been a lengthy, although on the whole amicable, discussion that afternoon. All the town's major citizens had assembled and the same gang leaders had arrived on hearing of Emma's party's return. Once again the blonde had told her story, being ably backed by Giselle. The little brunette had confirmed the details and added others that only she, as the "victim" of a kidnapping plot, could have known.

Maybe the story would not have received credence but for

two factors. If the women and the Texans had stolen money
for their own ends, they would have been unlikely to return.
That aspect had been mentioned and accepted. The second
item went unsaid, but nobody wanted to cast doubts with Ed
Caxton and his brother Matt hovering close at hand. None of
the audience had even offered to inquire why the two Texans
had taken the trouble to shave off their beards during the
time spent away from Hell.

Of course, things might not have gone so smoothly if the
various gang leaders and other depositors in Lampart's
"bank" had been the losers out of the robbery. Faced with
the threat of the outlaws going on the rampage to recoup
their looted money, the people of the town had formed a pot
and paid them off in full. So what would have been the most
dangerous element of opposition, the visiting fugitives from
justice, had seen no reason to cross trails or lock horns with a
pair of deadly efficient gunfighters like the Caxtons.

Having accepted that any hostile moves would have to be
carried out by themselves, the townspeople had been inclined to accept Emma's story. With that decision made, the
two factions had vied with each other for gaining the support
of the blonde's party. All had given their agreement to
Giselle assuming her dead husband's duties, with the proviso
that she allowed the committee to audit and have access to
the Civic Improvement Fund on its return. Dusty and the
women had agreed, promising that they would collect the
"buried money" on the morning after the allocation of
the ammunition to the *Kweharehnuh*.

Eventually the meeting had broken up, with everybody
apparently on the best of terms. One jarring note, soon
ended, had come when Emma had ordered Rosie Wilson to
quit the saloon and take her employees along. However,
finding that she no longer commanded support in her claims
to ownership, the brothelkeeper had yielded to the inevitable and obeyed.

The saloon's original staff had shown their delight at finding Emma reestablished as their boss. Setting to work willingly, they had given the building a thorough cleaning. By

sundown, the Honest Man had once more become the elegant, well-run place it had always been under the blonde's guidance.

To prevent the chance of smoke rising and giving away the location of the town, there was a strictly enforced ruling that no fires could be lit in the daytime. So Hell did not come to full life until after darkness had made possible the cooking of food. Several outlaws had pulled out following the destruction of the ammunition to avoid the wrath of the *Kwehareh-nuh,* which they had felt was sure to come. There were still a number of visitors and business at the saloon was satisfactory.

"Will Giselle be joining us?" Goldberg inquired, glancing at the stairs that led to the first floor.

"I don't think so," Emma replied. "She said that she intended to take a bath and grab some sleep."

Although the mayor's home had been ransacked after the discovery of Lampart's body, it had still been habitable. However, the little brunette had been vehement in her refusal to stay there. In the interests of peace and quiet, Emma had agreed to let Giselle share her quarters above the Honest Man's barroom. The blonde had felt that she was acting for the best. Knowing her half sister very well, Emma did not trust her and preferred to have her under observation.

"We'll be able to put on the usual show for Ten Bears tomorrow?" Crouch asked after a moment.

"Well, Giselle says that the box's all right as far as she can tell," the blonde answered. "The trouble is that she's got nobody to help her. She says that it needs somebody who knows the trick."

"And none of us knows it!" Connolly breathed, darting a nervous glance around the table. "Damn it! I always knew somebody should have learned how to do it from Simmy."

"They did," Emma announced calmly.

"Who?" demanded the three townsmen, all in the same breath.

"Me," the blonde told them, and sat back enjoying the sensation she had created. "Simmy taught me how and we had something rigged between us in case he wasn't able to do it for any reason."

"None of us knew that," Crouch said in an aggrieved tone.

"We never needed for me to do it before," Emma pointed out. "Hey. Where's Happy? Don't tell me that he's embalming those two yahoos Ed and Matt killed?"

"Embalming?" Goldberg put in, throwing a puzzled look from the blonde to Connolly.

"Isn't that what an undertaker does when he's getting a body ready to be buried?" Emma asked, oozing innocence. "You boys'll never believe it, but I had one as an admirer back East. I didn't know how he earned his living, mind, and when I found out, I dropped him fast."

"He's probably at Rosie's," Crouch commented. "Happy, I mean, not your undertaker friend from the East, Emma."

"She can probably use the business," the blonde smiled, hoping that the dangerous subject would drop. "The damned nerve of that woman, trying to take over my place."

"There were some who agreed that she should," Crouch replied.

"Are you hinting at something?" Goldberg demanded indignantly, seeing the jeweler's words as an attempt to undermine himself with the blonde's faction. "I didn't hear *you* objecting to it."

"Shucks, you boys weren't to know what had happened." Emma smiled, satisfied that her slip of the tongue had been laid aside, if not forgotten. "Rosie always was a pushy woman. Let's have a drink to the future prosperity of Hell. And this one's on me."

Wearing nothing but a pair of long-john underpants, Emmet Youseman sat nursing a naked, pretty brunette employee of Rosie Wilson's brothel. There was a partially filled glass in his hand and an almost empty bottle of whiskey on the dressing table, which along with the bed and a chair formed the small room's furnishings. Male and female clothes lay in an untidy pile on the floor, discarded by the couple on their arrival earlier in the evening.

The girl had long since become adept at persuading her

customers to drink more than was good for them, while remaining sober herself. That night she had paid an even
greater attention to her task, for she had been given orders
by her employer. However, despite being very far gone in
liquor, Youseman still showed no inclination of giving her
the required information.

"You've got a fine mammary protuberance there, Peggy,"
the undertaker announced with drunken gravity, his free
hand jiggling one of her jutting breasts. "Let'sh go 'n' lie
down so I can examine it some more."

"Aw, Happy," the girl protested. "You was telling me how
you and Doc Connolly took care of them dead fellers.
What'd you need Doc there for, seeing's they was both of
'em dead?"

"Huh?" grunted Youseman, and finished his drink with a
single gulp. "Why, that'sh a she- . . . shecret, Peggy."

"Gee, Happy," the girl protested, knowing that he was fast
approaching the point where he would collapse in a drunken
stupor. "It's not right that you keep secrets from li'l ole me."

"I shupposesh not," Youseman muttered, still fondling the
breast. "You . . . a good girl, Peggy. Only that miserable
old bash- . . . my esteemed and respected partner . . .
Isn't he the most misherable old bashtard you've ever met?"

"Sure he is," Peggy agreed. "And he's not worth keeping
any ole secret for, is he?"

"No, shiree," the undertaker mumbled, lurching to his feet
and letting the girl slide from his lap. "Le'sh go bed 'n' I
tell."

An angry curse broke from Peggy's lips as she watched the
burly undertaker staggering unevenly across the room. All
too well she recognized the symptoms and knew that her
boss would gain no further information that night. Falling
heavily onto the bed, Youseman lay snorting like a pig as he
dropped into an unassailable drunken sleep. Obviously, Rosie Wilson had been eavesdropping at the door. Its drapes
jerked open and the woman entered.

"The drunken, useless pig!" the big woman snarled, cross-

ing to the bed and delivering a stinging slap to Youseman's
face.

"It wasn't my fault!" Peggy yelped, wishing to exculpate
herself. "You know he never talks about anything important
until he's nearly ready to go under from the drink."

"I know," Rosie confirmed. "Get dressed and go out
front. There're some fellers wanting company and a roll in
the hay. What you make, you can keep."

"Gee, thanks, Rosie!" the girl enthused, and started to
sort out her clothes.

While the girl dressed, not a lengthy affair, Rosie searched
the undertaker's pockets. The woman let out a low hiss of
excitement as she produced two door keys.

"Leave him sleep here," Rosie commanded, not troubling
to hide her excitement at the find. "Maybe you'd better stay
with him and make sure he doesn't leave if he wakes."

"Aw, Rosie . . . !" Peggy began, seeing her chance of a
fee slipping away.

"I'll cover what you'd've made from those fellers," the
brothelkeeper promised. "And mind, you keep your mouth
shut about this."

"You can count on it," the girl assured her employer's
departing back.

Going through the customer's lounge at the front of the
building, Rosie entered and locked the connecting door of
her private office. At her desk, she produced a Smith & Wesson No. 3 American revolver and bull's-eye lantern. Setting
them down with the two keys, she collected and donned the
long black cloak that hung on a hook behind the parlor's
door. After lighting the lantern, but covering its lens, she left
by the side entrance. Peering cautiously around, she made
her way between the *jacales* and toward the rear of the undertaker's place of business.

Rosie had often suspected that Youseman and Connolly
were involved in clandestine activities outside, yet in some
way connected with, their respective lines of employment.
Previously, when very drunk, the undertaker had hinted as
much, but had always avoided saying exactly what they

might be. Having noticed how the pair had reacted that afternoon to the comments of Emma Nene and the Caxton brothers about exhumations, her suspicions had grown even stronger.

Actually, the two men's behavior had merely strengthened the brothelkeeper's theory of what their activities might be. One earlier attempt to unearth it—literally as well as figuratively—had come to nothing. The man she had sent—an impoverished outlaw—to open up a grave had been shot by somebody who had seen him about to commence his work. While Rosie's part in the affair had not been detected, she had come no closer to solving the mystery.

Still trying to obtain knowledge that might prove profitable, the woman had ordered Peggy to try to worm it from Youseman. On every occasion, he had fallen into a drunken sleep without yielding his secret. While he had always carried the key to his premises' rear door, it had availed Rosie nothing. It had given her access only to his living quarters. Her searches of them had not produced the means of entering the building's business section. With the second key in her possession, she hoped to be able to carry her investigations into the previously protected regions.

If the secret had been sufficiently important—or potentially dangerous—to make Connolly and Youseman instantly compliant with the demands of the saloonkeeper and the Texans, it ought to be worth the effort taken to learn it. Rosie had never rated high on the town's social scale. The other citizens, no matter how loathsome the crimes that had driven them to Hell, had always tended to look down on her. Having access to information that would put the two men under her domination would go far toward changing the situation.

Entering Youseman's establishment, the woman tried the second key in the lock on the inner door. It worked and she passed through into the laying-out room.

Earlier that day, the bodies of the Texans' victims had been displayed there in their coffins for anybody who wished to come and pay their last respects. Rosie had been one of the few to attend and had watched the lids of the coffins screwed firmly into place. Although Youseman had ushered her and a couple more mourners out into the waiting carriage, he would not have had time to unscrew the lids and remove the bodies before the coffins were carried from the room and into the hearse.

Frowning, Rosie directed the beam of her lantern onto the sturdy bench upon which the coffins were always placed for the last visits. She saw nothing at first, and its stout wooden front prevented her from looking underneath. Then her attention was attracted by a slightly protruding knot in the timber. She pressed and felt it give, but nothing else happened. Still certain that she was on the verge of making a discovery, she began to press the top of the bench where one of the coffins had been resting. Silently but smoothly, an oblong section of the top hinged down from its further narrow end. It was only down for a few seconds and rose again of its own volition.

Pressing again, Rosie directed the beam of her lantern into the cavity. It illuminated a section of the building's basement and another bench immediately below her. Hardened as she might be, Rosie could not hold back a startled gasp nor resist withdrawing hurriedly. The trapdoor closed automatically.

But not before Rosie had seen the two vaguely human forms, swathed in tarpaulin, that lay on the basement's bench.

"So that's what your game is, huh!" Rosie breathed. "Now we'll see who's so high and mighty."

Making sure that she left no traces of her visit, the woman walked from the laying-out room. Having locked both doors behind her, she stepped warily away from the building. Give them their due, Youseman and Connolly had come up with a real smart way of retaining possession of bodies. Nobody who had seen the coffin's lid secured would have suspected that its bottom opened and deposited the corpse into the basement. Those Chinese laborers brought in by Li Chin of the Oriental laundry—and once a prominent Tong leader, who had been put on the run after a race war—would have built the basement. Probably Simeon Lampart was the designer of the trapdoors. A scheme such as the two men were carrying out could only have succeeded with the mayor's assistance and authority.

Rosie could not decide just to what purpose she could put her knowledge. Yet she felt certain that she could reap some advantage from it. Even if the two men were of no use, the outlaw leaders might find the information interesting.

Wanting time to think out a line of action, she strolled along the rear of the buildings flanking the main street. She continued to move cautiously, keeping to the shadows. Hinges squeaked, and a cloaked and hooded figure emerged furtively from the back door of the combined barbershop and bathhouse. Beyond guessing that the shape was feminine and small, Rosie could gain no clue to its identity.

Giving a shrug, Rosie walked slowly on. Since the death of its owner, the barbershop had been kept in operation by his assistant. The brothelkeeper had never considered that the young man would make a worthwhile ally. So she felt little interest in his private affairs. She would have strolled straight by the open door, but a male voice from the darkened interior reached her ears.

"You acted in a stupid manner, my gauche young friend. Only a fool would have believed the story she told to you and trusted her. I'll admit that she is very easy to believe and trust. I did so once myself. Well, you are dead. But the price you have paid for your folly was, I think, less than mine."

Hearing footsteps approaching the door, Rosie looked around. The female visitor had already gone from sight and there did not appear to be any other witnesses in the vicinity. If murder had been done, which seemed likely going by what she had heard, she might be able to turn a profit out of it. The voice had been that of an educated man, an Easterner, yet not one she recognized. If it should be one of the citizens, the possibilities of blackmail were worth Rosie taking a few chances.

Raising and cocking her Smith & Wesson, she pointed it at the doorway. At the same time she leveled the bull's-eye lantern, ready for use. A tall shape materialized before her, coming to a halt on catching sight of the woman.

"Don't move, feller!" Rosie commanded, flicking open the front of the lantern. "I'll shoot if you do."

As far as the brothelkeeper could discern, the shape in the doorway was male. He had on a top hat, from beneath which long, reddish hair flowed to disappear beneath the black cloak that his left arm held up in front of his face.

"Good evening," the man greeted politely, without offering to lower the cloak. "And a pleasant one—"

"Put your arm down so I can see your face," Rosie interrupted.

"I would rather you didn't see it," answered the man.

"That's likely, but I aim to," Rosie replied, a little scared by his attitude and the glint in the hollow eyes that showed between the top of the cloak and the brim of the high hat. "Damn you, I'll sh—"

"You won't shoot me, madam," the man declared, and carried out her order.

Instantly Rosie stiffened and her face showed horror at what had been exposed to the lantern's light. The man's right hand emerged from the folds of the cloak. It held a Remington Double Deringer. Even as Rosie's mouth opened to let out a shriek of terror, flame blossomed from the little gun's uppermost barrel. Hit below the left breast by the .41-caliber bullet, the woman reeled and the lantern's glow flickered away from the man's face. Rosie fired once, the revolver sounding loudly and driving its load into the side of the building harmlessly. Again the man's pistol spat and the second ball plowed its way into the staggering woman's body. She dropped the lantern and the Smith & Wesson, crumpling down herself. From the street, shouts sounded and feet thudded as people came to investigate the shooting.

"I said I'd rather not show you my face," the man commented, and turned to stride away into the darkness.

Five minutes later, Dusty Fog knelt at the stricken woman's side. Connolly had done what little he could to save her, but he had warned the small Texan that she would not last much longer.

On his arrival, accompanied by members of the Civic Regulators, Dusty had taken charge of the affair. Leaving Connolly to attend to the woman, the small Texan, Waco, Goldberg, and Crouch had entered the barbershop. They found its new owner sprawled facedown on the floor in the living quarters. He was dead, knifed through the heart. There had been no signs of a struggle, nor anything to suggest why he had been killed.

From his examination of the outside, Dusty had concluded that Rosie surprised the killer rather than being the guilty party herself. She had no knife on her, nor had one been found in the vicinity. The lantern and the Smith & Wesson revolver with one chamber discharged had given strength to his theory. So he wanted, if possible, to learn what the woman had seen.

"Did you know the man who shot you, ma'am?" Dusty asked gently.

"M-man . . . !" Rosie answered, turning agony-distorted features to the small Texan. "H-his . . . f-face . . ."

"What about it?" Dusty prompted in the same quiet tone.

"H-he . . . didn't . . . have . . . a . . . face . . . !" the woman almost shrieked. Blood burst from her mouth, her body convulsed briefly and then went limp.

13
MY MEDICINE WILL STRIKE
YOU DOWN

Spread-eagled back downward, with wrists and ankles secured to stakes driven firmly into the ground, the Ysabel Kid peered through the gloom toward the conical roof of the *tipi* above him. He was forced to admit that he could only blame himself for his present predicament. Which did not make him feel any better about being in it.

Having ended the second duel, he had known that he could not stay longer in the *Kweharehnuhs'* village. Not only did convention demand that he should leave, but he had felt sure that *Pohawe* would make other attempts to remove him if he stayed. For some reason or other, the woman wanted him dead. So, having no wish to be forced into more duels or to be poisoned by *Pohawe* if she could not find further challengers, he had announced his departure.

Understanding at least part of the Kid's motives and approving of them, Ten Bears had given his consent for the Texan to leave. However, the dance had not been canceled.

It was to continue, even though its guest-of-honor would no longer be present. From comments the Kid had heard passed during the afternoon, the allocation of ammunition was to take place the following day. That, too, had been an inducement to continue with the celebrations.

While collecting his property from Wolf Runner's *tipi*, the Kid had heard enough to warn him that the allocation might not be peaceful. The braves started chanting the words of the *Kweharehnuh* war song, then a warrior had interrupted the singing to recount the story of his greatest, bravest deed. Taken with all he had seen earlier, the Kid had known that he must not delay in taking a warning to Dusty. Unless the allocation went off without a hitch, the braves would commence an attack.

The Kid had been struck down and captured on the outskirts of the village. Hurtling from a *tipi*'s entrance, an all-but-naked brave had tackled him around the knees. Before he could resist, three more had pounced upon him. The back of a tomahawk's head had collided with his skull and he had known no more until recovering in what his nose had warned was the *tipi* of the medicine woman.

Going by the reduced volume of noise from the dance, the *tipi* was situated some distance from the village. That figured. A medicine man or woman often set up an establishment well clear of other human habitations, to permit a greater secrecy and increased freedom to carry out his, or her, duties.

The Kid was alone in the *tipi*, but he knew that it did not greatly enhance his chances of escape. Having already tested the strength and security of his bonds, he knew that he could achieve little or nothing against them. A slow and painful death lay ahead for him—and for many of the people at Hell —if he could not regain his freedom.

A memory stirred at the back of the Kid's mind, prodded into life by his realization of where he was being held prisoner. On the night before he had ridden away on his first war trail—to join the Confederate States' Army—he had been visited by the *Pehnanes'* respected senior medicine woman. She had been the midwife who had attended his birth and had subsequently taken a great interest in his welfare and career.

"If you are ever in medicine trouble, *Cuchilo,*" she had said, "call on me no matter where you are and I will help you."

Well, the Kid figured that he could say he was in medicine trouble. Just about as deep and dangerous as a *Pehnane tehnap* could get. Relaxing as much as his bonds would permit, he turned his eyes toward the apex of the *tipi.*

"Raccoon Talker!" he gritted, from deep down in his chest. *"Cuchilo* needs your help!"

Again and again he repeated the words, while sweat bathed his face and soaked his clothes. If there had been a witness present and able to see, he would have been amazed at the strain of concentration showing on the babyishly innocent dark brown face.

Close to four hundred miles away, at the reservation agent's home on the lower slopes of Mount Scott in the Indian Nations, two thrilled, middle-aged white women were having their fortunes told by a genuine Comanche medicine woman.

Carefully selected for his post, liked, respected, and trusted by the Comanche bands under his care, Agent Stanley Beckers was not the kind of man to allow exploitation of his charges. That he had given permission for Raccoon Talker to see the women was a tribute on his part to the man who had made the request. Few white men could have persuaded Long Walker, now *paria:vo* of the *Pehnane* band, to ask such a favor of the medicine woman. Stocky, bearded, almost Comanche in build, the rancher, who wore a vest made from the hide of a cattle-killing jaguar that had raided his herds, was such a man. His name was Charles Goodnight.

In addition to showing a pair of influential Eastern cattle buyers some excellent sport and hunting, Goodnight had found himself faced with the task of entertaining their wives.

Being close to the Comanche reservation, he had visited his old friend Long Walker and had been given the answer to his dilemma. The wives had been delighted for the opportunity to meet an Indian medicine woman and it had been a rather amused Raccoon Talker who suggested that she should tell their fortunes.

Suddenly Raccoon Talker stopped speaking. She broke off her conventional phrases—which had been basically the same as those employed by fortune-tellers of every nation, creed, or cult—abruptly and without apparent reason. Stiffening on her seat, she stared with fixed intensity across the room. Her face set into lines of intense concentration and she showed signs of being under a tremendous mental strain.

"Wha-what's wrong with her, Charles?" gasped one of the white women, rising hurriedly and displaying alarm.

"I don't know," Goodnight admitted, looking at the buxom, white-haired, yet impressive figure in the spotlessly clean doeskin clothes and the finery of her profession. In fluent Comanche, employing the accent of the *Tanima*— Liver Eater—band, he went on, "Is all well with Raccoon Talker, brother?"

"Keep quiet, *Chaqueta Tigre,*" Long Walker requested politely. "Tell your women not to be alarmed. There is medicine power here and it is no longer a foolish game for the squaws."

Goodnight nodded and passed on the information. To give them their due, the plump Eastern matrons fell silent. Each of them realized that she was participating in something of more importance than a mere fortune-telling exercise such as they could have received from a gypsy peddler back home in New Jersey. For his part, the rancher knew they were witnessing something unique.

During the war between the states, while riding with Captain Jack Cureton's company of Texas Rangers, Goodnight had learned much about the Comanches and something of their religious beliefs. So he had a slight inkling of what might be happening. It had been during that same period he

had won his *Nemenuh* man-name, *Chaqueta Tigre,* Jaguar
Coat, by his courage and his always wearing that distinctive
vest.

For almost three minutes Raccoon Talker sat as if turned
to stone. Only the increased rate at which her bosom rose
and fell, in sympathy with her deep breathing, showed that
she was still alive. No sound came from her and a deep silence dropped over the room. Then the glazed expression
left her face and her eyes took on a new light of animation.
Coming to her feet, she inclined her head in response to the
white women's exclamations of concern.

"I must go," Raccoon Talker declared. "*Cuchilo* has need
of my help, Long Walker, and I cannot give it in this place."

"Give the paleface chiefs' squaws our apologies, *Chaqueta
Tigre,* as you white men do such foolish things," the stocky,
gray-haired *paria:vo* of the *Pehnane* requested, showing
none of the anxiety that had been caused by the medicine
woman's words. "But we must leave this place."

"We need no apologies, brother," Goodnight replied. "Is
there anything I can do to help? As you know, I owe your
tawk[1] a debt and he is my friend."

Colonel Goodnight—the military title was honorary,
granted by virtue of his courage, reliability, and powers of
leadership—had never been a man to ignore a friend in trouble nor to forget to repay a debt. All too well he knew just
how much the success of his first big cattle drive across the
Llano Estacado—which had helped pave the way for the
economic recovery of Texas—had been due to the Kid's
knowledge and assistance.[2]

"Yes," Raccoon Talker put in. "Send word over the singing wires to the *paria:vo* of the Texans. *Cuchilo* says the time
has come. The blue-coats must ride to the Palo Duro."

"That I will do," Goodnight confirmed. "Is there anything
more?"

1. *Tawk:* Comanche word meaning both grandfather and grandson.
2. Told in: *Goodnight's Dream* and *From Hide and Horn.*

"I think not," the woman answered, and turned from the table. "The rest is medicine, *Chaqueta Tigre.*"

"That I understand," agreed the rancher, and crossed to open the door with all the gallantry he would have displayed to the governor's wife or a saloon girl.

"We will make medicine this night, Agent Beckers," Long Walker announced, as Raccoon Talker left the room. "Tell the soldier-coats at the fort there is nothing to fear from our drumming."

"I will tell them," the agent promised. "I know your heart is strong for peace, my brother."

"What's happening?" asked the wife of the senior cattle buyer, after the Comanches had taken their departure and the rapid drumming of horses' hooves had faded away.

"It's a personal matter, ma'am," Goodnight explained. "Long Walker told me to express his apologies for them having to leave so abruptly."

"But why did they have to leave?" the second woman inquired.

"Raccoon Talker heard that a young friend of ours needs help," the rancher replied. "She's gone to give it."

"I didn't hear anything," the first wife protested.

"Neither did I, ma'am," Goodnight assured her. "The Comanche medicine people have powers that no white person can understand. If you will accept Mr. Becker's hospitality for a short time longer, I have business to which I must attend. Stanley, I'll deliver the message to the fort."

"Sure, Charlie," Beckers agreed. "I don't know what's going on, but I *do* know we'd better do what Raccoon Talker said we should."

Despite having been born and raised among the *Pehnane,* the Kid had little actual knowledge of medicine powers. They were the prerogative of the elite few, mostly older men or women. If a young person showed the correct gifts, he or she would be chosen for training and introduction to the medicine arts. Mostly the male candidate would be of a mild, dreamy nature and unlikely ever to gain acclaim in the martial subjects. From his youngest days, the Kid had been marked down as a warrior. So he had learned of medicine as an outsider, knowing only what it was claimed those in the inner circle could do.

How it had happened, the Kid could not say, but he knew that Raccoon Talker had "heard" his message. More than that, he was certain that she had promised him her assistance and protection. Settling himself as comfortably as possible under the circumstances, he waited for the next development.

A lantern glowed and footsteps approached the *tipi*. Its door flaps were opened to let in a flood of light. Followed by a trio of war-painted *tehnaps, Pohawe* strode into the Kid's presence. Having looked at the newcomers, the Kid devoted his attention to his surroundings. In addition to the usual paraphernalia of a medicine *tipi*, he saw that all his portable property had been brought in. The rifle, still in its medicine boot, leaned against his saddle and his gun belt, carrying its usual armament, lay across its seat. At the opposite side of the *tipi,* encased in a medicine boot, leaned a long Sharps Model of 1859 rifle.

The latter weapon must be in the *tipi* so that it could absorb medicine power. Yet a rifle rarely received such treatment. Obviously it must be required for some special purpose.

"What evil is this, witch-woman?" the Kid demanded, swinging coldly contemptuous eyes toward *Pohawe.*

Anger showed on the woman's face, brought there by the name that the Kid had applied to her. While a medicine woman was a person to be respected, a witch—who used her powers for evil—was regarded with revulsion.

"You die, *Cuchilo,*" *Pohawe* promised. "Not this night, but after the sun has gone down tomorrow, you will go to join your white father. There will be no living palefaces in the Palo Duro. I will not have them here."

"Does a woman lead the *Kweharehnuh?*" the Kid mocked, looking at the braves. "Are the Antelopes like the foolish men in the Land Of The Grandmother,[3] waiting to be led by a warrior maid with a war lance?"[4]

"He talks well, *Pohawe,*" snorted the biggest of the *tehnaps.* When he moved forward, he exhibited a very bad limp to his left leg. "We will see if he dies well—"

"Not this night, Kills From Far Off," the medicine woman barked.

"Why wait, witch-woman?" challenged the Kid. "Are you afraid that my medicine will strike you down?"

"What dog of a half-breed ever had medicine?" *Pohawe* snorted.

"I know a half-breed *bitch* who *thinks* she has," replied the Kid.

For a moment, the Texan thought that he had pushed *Pohawe* too far. Rage twisted her features into almost bestial lines. Her hand reached toward the knife at a *tehnap*'s waist. Then, with a visible effort of will, she relaxed.

"It is well for you that I have chosen the time and how you are to die, half-breed. I want you alive to hear of the great thing I have done and will do."

"Then kill me now, witch-woman," challenged the Kid. "Your words tire me and you will do no deeds worth listening to."

"You think not?" *Pohawe* screeched. "I am the one who will guide the *Nemenuh* as they drive the palefaces from Comancheria."

"The *Kweharehnuh* are good warriors, those who are not led by a witch-woman," the Kid told her. "But I don't think they can drive out the white people."

"The other bands will ride with us," the medicine woman stated.

"You couldn't have been at the Fort Sorrell peace meeting," drawled the Kid. "The chiefs of the other bands were wise enough to know that not even the *Nemenuh* could win

3. Land of the Grandmother: Canada during the reign of Queen Victoria.
4. More details of this legend are given in: *The Whip and the War Lance.*

victory against the wheel guns of the soldier-coats. So they made an honorable peace and will keep it."

"They were old fools and cowards, all of them!" *Pohawe* snapped. "And their braves did not have many rifles. Every *Kweharehnuh* warrior carries a repeater and has bullets for it. Tomorrow we will have many more bullets. With them, we can fight and beat the soldier-coats. As for their slow wheel guns, they are only good for shooting from far away at the *tipis* standing still in a village."

"When the news goes out that the *Kweharehnuh* are counting many coups and bringing in much loot," Kills From Far Off continued, "the bravehearts eating the white man's beef on the reservations will ride swiftly to join us."

Looking from the *tehnap* to the woman, the Kid managed to school his expression into one of amused disbelief. Yet, in his heart, he knew that they had been speaking the truth. Armed with repeaters against the Springfield single-shot rifles and carbines with which the U.S. Army was equipped, the *Kweharehnuhs* would have a decided advantage in fire-power. Nor would batteries of cannon be of any great use against a highly mobile force of attacking braves who, knowing every inch of the terrain, would select with care the places from which they launched their assaults.

What was more, the couple had been correct in their summation of how the news would be received by the restless young braves on the reservation. They would be determined to share in the *Kweharehnuh*'s glory. So the very thing that Governor Howard had feared and that the floating outfit had come to Hell to try to avert—a bloody, costly Indian war— would have to be fought. Certainly many people of both races would be slaughtered if *Pohawe* had her way.

Ever since the challenges by the two brothers had been issued, the Kid had sensed that they were instigated by *Pohawe.* At last he could see possible motives for her wishing to have him killed. On learning of his arrival in the village, she must have come to the wrong conclusions concerning the reason for his visit. She could have believed that some hint of her plans had leaked out and he had been sent in an attempt to persuade Ten Bears to stay at peace—if only nominally—with the white people. Or she had suspected that the Kid was connected with Hell and had not wanted word of the preparations being made for war to be carried to the citizens.

In either case, she would have wanted him out of the way and the brothers' hatred had offered her the means. Maybe she had talked them into the belief that they must avenge their brother. The plan had gone wrong for her, but she clearly did not intend to let things go at that.

There was only one hope for the Kid: that his faith in Raccoon Talker's medicine powers would be justified.

"The bravehearts on the reservations won't follow you," the Kid warned, trying to sound a whole heap more confident than he felt. "Not when you, like them, depend on the white men for weapons and ammunition."

"That will not be so after tomorrow," *Pohawe* replied, and the other three *tehnaps* directed knowing grins at Kills From Far Off.

"*Paruwa Semenho* is a man of honor," the Kid stated. "If the white people keep their bargain, so will he."

"They will not keep *all* of their bargain," the woman countered. "There will be no pretended making of medicine tomorrow."

"*Pretended?*" queried the Kid. "I have heard it said that the great witch-woman of the *Kweharehnuh* does not know how such medicine is made."

"It is false medicine," declared the youngest *tehnap*.

"So the witch-woman tells you," answered the Kid. "But that is because she doesn't understand it. Perhaps *she* does not have true medicine power herself."

"You are asking to die, *Cuchilo!*" *Pohawe* hissed, playing into his hands.

"Then have me killed," the Kid suggested. "I say you can't, because I am protected by a greater power than you know. Try to kill me, witch-woman, and see if I speak with a crooked tongue."

"Kill him, One Arrow!" the woman spat at the youngest *tehnap*.

"Try it if you dare, *namae'enuh,*"[5] jeered the Kid, using the most insulting term in the Comanches' vocabulary as he saw the brave hesitate.

There ought to have been sufficient time for Raccoon Talker to have made her medicine. If not, going by One Arrow's response to the deadly insult, the Kid could count himself lucky if he stayed alive long enough to come under her promised protection.

Spitting out a curse, the young *tehnap* snatched his knife from its sheath. Watched by his companions and the medicine woman, he took two strides in the Texan's direction. Then he stopped as if he had run into an invisible wall. Fright and shock contorted his face and he collapsed in what looked like a fit.

Startled exclamations burst from the other men and they backed away involuntarily. Brave enough in the face of mortal dangers, they were unnerved by the manifestation of powers beyond their understanding. One Arrow was known to suffer from such seizures, but the attack had come on just too conveniently for it to be discounted on natural grounds.

"Kill him, Small Post Oak!" *Pohawe* screeched, sounding frightened.

"Not me!" the brave addressed by the woman replied. "Come, brothers. We will leave this place."

Snatching up the Sharps rifle, Kills From Far Off followed his companions as they dragged One Arrow from the *tipi*. *Pohawe* watched them go, seething with fury, yet shivering with fear.

"*Cuchilo!*" the woman hissed, glaring her hatred but keeping her distance. "If those men won't follow me tomorrow, I will return and kill you slowly. And if I come, no medicine power will save you."

5. *Namae'enuh:* put politely, he who has had incestuous intercourse."

14
MY NAME *IS* DUSTY FOG

"Young Duprez had been knifed," Dusty Fog told Emma Nene as they stood away from other ears in the Honest Man saloon. "Rosie Wilson had been shot outside the back door, but I think she'd run into the killer, not that she killed him."

"Had he been robbed?" the blonde inquired, glancing at the ceiling.

"There wasn't any sign of it," Dusty admitted. "Why'd you think he might have been?"

"There doesn't seem to be any other reason for him to be killed," Emma answered, just a shade too emphatically. "He wasn't a prominent citizen, or an important asset to any of the cliques. Nobody else, that I know of, can handle the barbering. So he wasn't killed to let somebody else take over the business. That doesn't leave much else but robbery, does it?"

"Was he a ladies' man? They do say those French fellers mostly are."

"I don't think Paul Duprez could even speak French. His folks were born in Brooklyn. Anyways, when he used to come in here, I've never seen any of the girls trampling over each other to get to him. I'll ask around for you."

"*Gracias,*" Dusty drawled.

"*Es nada,*" Emma answered, forcing a smile to her lips. "It could have been one of Rosie's girls, though. Her being outside and all."

"Like you say," Dusty replied. "It could be."

Watching the blonde, the small Texan could sense that she was deeply disturbed by the news. Her eyes repeatedly flickered toward the first floor and, in a controlled way, she was agitated by what she had just heard.

Then Dusty remembered something that he had been told about Duprez's late employer. Jean le Blanc had been a society barber in the East, until he had been persuaded by a woman he had thought loved him to murder her millionaire husband. Too late, he had learned that she was merely using him to open the way for herself and her real lover. He had killed the couple and carried off a large sum of money and a valuable collection of jewelry they had been meaning to use in their life together.

Emma Nene and Giselle Lampart had known le Blanc's life story—and the reason for their return to Hell had been to lay hands on a fortune in jewelry.

"Where's Giselle?" Dusty asked, watching carefully for reactions.

"Upstairs, of course," the blonde replied, a hint of alarm dancing in eyes that were a whole heap more expressive than she imagined. "Why?"

"She went to the bathhouse. Maybe she saw or heard something."

"It's not likely. She was there as soon as the baths were ready."

"Did you see her come back?"

"Yes," Emma lied. "When I went out to check on the liquor supply. She came in the back way and went straight upstairs."

"Uh-huh!" Dusty grunted noncommittally.

"Where's Wa- . . . Matt?" the blonde inquired in an obvious attempt to change the subject.

"He went with Goldberg and Connolly to the cathouse."

"I didn't think Manny or the esteemed doctor went in for *that* kind of entertainment."

"I wouldn't know," Dusty admitted. "We found a couple of keys in Rosie's pocket and I want to know what locks they fit. She was away from her place and I don't see her as the kind who'd take a walk just for the good of her complexion."

"I suppose not." The blonde smiled.

"Maybe I'd best go and talk to Giselle, anyways," Dusty remarked.

"You're the boss," Emma declared, hoping that the sinking sensation in her stomach was not openly obvious. "But I don't think you'll learn anything from her."

At the brothel, Waco, Goldberg, and Connolly were being confronted by the big, brawny bouncer. Half a dozen Chinese, Mexican, and white girls hovered nervously in the background. One of the latter was staring at the blond youngster with a puzzled expression on her face.

"Where's Mr. Youseman?" Goldberg demanded pompously.

"Who says he's here?" countered the bouncer.

"We *know* he is," the hotelkeeper declared. "And we want to see him immediately."

"Rosie said that she don't take to the marks being disturbed," the bouncer answered. "It's bad for the girls, getting stopped halfway through. So you can't go and see him."

"Now me," Waco drawled, "I don't rightly see any way you-all can stop us. These gents're mighty important citizens and members of the Civic Regulators and, top of that, there's me—"

"You?" the bouncer said, showing his puzzlement.

"Me," confirmed Waco, right-hand Colt flashing from its holster and its hammer going back to full cock. "And this."

The instantaneous response robbed the bouncer of any further inclination to resist. Not only—as the blond Texan had pointed out—was he dealing with two mighty influential members of the community, but he was facing Matt Caxton, younger brother of the most deadly *pistolero* ever to arrive in Hell and no slouch with a gun on his own account. With Rosie absent—the man still did not know of her death—he lacked guidance and figured that he had better cooperate. If only to save his own life.

"Aw, I didn't mean nothing!" the bouncer stated, with an ingratiating grin. "You'll find him in the third back room. Only, way he is, he'll not be any use for undertaking to-night."

Going to the third of the rooms used by the girls and their clients, Waco's party discovered the truth of the bouncer's words. Youseman lay in his drunken stupor, but Peggy was awake and talkative. On learning of the reason for the visit, she admitted that her late employer had taken Youseman's keys with the intention of visiting and searching his premises.

Waco had already guessed that the doctor had recognized the keys. Anger showed on Connolly's miserable face, mingled with considerable alarm. Going by the other's reactions, Waco figured that he had made a smart and correct guess.

"Why would Rosie want to search a funeral parlor?" Goldberg demanded.

"I dunno," Peggy lied, holding back the full extent of her knowledge in the hope that it might later be turned to her advantage. "She just wanted to, is all she told me. You don't argue with Rosie when she tells you to do something."

"What did she tell you to do?" Connolly gritted.

"Get him drunk, is all," Peggy replied.

Watching the girl, Waco sensed that she was not speaking the whole truth. He also decided that he would let her reasons for lying go unquestioned for the moment. Dusty's purposes were better served right then by preventing an exposure of the undertaker's and doctor's second line of business.

"Youseman always had plenty of money around the place," Connolly remarked, as Goldberg seemed to be on the verge of asking another question. He had no desire for the investigation to dig further into the brothelkeeper's motives. "She probably planned to rob him."

"By cracky, doc," Waco enthused. "I reckon you've hit it. We'd best go see if she got in and took anything."

"I'll attend to that, Manny!" Connolly declared hastily. "There's no need for us all to go."

"I think it would be better if we all went," Goldberg answered. "Let's get going now. There's nothing more to be learned here."

"It'd be best if we all went, doc," Waco agreed, knowing that a refusal would increase any suspicions Goldberg might be harboring.

Although agreement entailed some risk, Waco felt that they were justified in taking it. Rosie Wilson had been a shrewd, smart woman. She would have removed all the evidence of her visit to the funeral parlor. She had not made it in the interests of public duty and would not wish for a prior exposure of her knowledge. So it was unlikely that the hotelkeeper would see anything that might tell of the undertaker's and doctor's dealings in human bodies.

"I think that we should send for Crouch to come and help us," Goldberg stated, as the trio left the brothel.

Since their clash of interests over who should run the town, a distinct coldness had risen between the former partners. So the words had been provoked by nothing more than Goldberg's objections to having to work while Crouch was doing nothing.

"There's no call for that," Connolly replied hurriedly. "We three ought to be able to handle things."

"Why sure," Waco agreed.

"Huh!" Goldberg sniffed. "I dare say *my* wife was alarmed by the shooting. But *I* didn't have to dash off and comfort her while other people do the work. Some of us have a sense of duty."

"He's got him a right pretty li'l wife," Waco commented soothingly, but without displaying too much tact.

"Wife!" Goldberg snorted. "I'd like to see the synagogue *they* were married in—"

Anything more the hotelkeeper might have felt like saying was stopped by the sight of a man running toward them. Coming up, he proved to be one of Emma's waiters and in a state of considerable excitement.

"*Señor* Caxton says come *pronto*," the man gasped. "*Señor* and *Señora* Crouch have been attacked and murdered."

Having reached his decision to visit Giselle, Dusty turned toward the stairs. Before he could leave Emma's side, there was an interruption. The batwing doors burst open and Crouch staggered in. Agony contorted his face and blood smeared his hands as they clasped on the gore-saturated front of his shirt at belly level. Reeling forward a few steps, he stood swaying and glaring around.

Racing across the barroom, Dusty caught Crouch as his legs buckled and he started to collapse. Gently easing the man into a sitting position, Dusty supported him against his bent knee. Pain-glazed eyes stared at the small Texan and he knew there would not be much time in which he could gather information.

"What happened?" Dusty inquired, then scowled at the people as they came crowding around. "Back off, some of you, damn it! Emma. Get them back to what they were doing, *pronto*. And send a man to fetch Doc Connolly."

It said much for the strength of the big Texan's personality that the onlookers drew away without Emma needing to do much prompting. Satisfied that his demands were being respected, Dusty raised no objections to the gang leaders and a couple of citizens hovering close by.

"B-Betty!" Crouch gasped, clutching at Dusty's right arm. "B-Bet . . . I found her d-dead. M-mur-murdered!"

"How?" Dusty asked, conscious of the mutters that arose from all around.

"W-with . . . knife . . . j-just . . . like . . . Duprez. M-man did . . . it."

"Which man?"

"Str-stranger t-to me. Ne-never seen him be . . . fore. He . . . knifed me as I turned to come . . . help."

"What did he look like?"

"Tall," Crouch croaked, clearly making every effort to think straight and give helpful facts. "He wore . . . top hat . . . had long hair. Had an . . . opera cloak on, couldn't see his other clothes."

"How about his face?" Dusty inquired gently.

"I . . . I . . . don't know," Crouch admitted. "L-light was behind him. Don't think he was anybody I know."

At that moment, Dusty saw O'Day come in through a side door. The man had not offered to continue the acquaintance they had struck up on the way to town. In fact, he had explained that he did not wish to become associated with any particular faction of Hell's society. In view of Giselle's obvious dislike of the Easterner, along with his own inclination, Dusty had not forced himself into O'Day's company. With the situation so unsettled, O'Day had not yet been required to make his contribution to the Civic Improvement Fund. Although he had taken a room at the hotel, he apparently had not followed the usual outlaw trend of purchasing fancy "go-to-town" clothes. Bareheaded, showing short brown hair that was going thin on top, he was dressed as when the floating outfit had saved his life.

"Did he say anything?" Dusty asked, turning his attention back to Crouch.

"N- . . . He . . . didn't spe- . . . !" the jeweler began, then a fit of coughing sprayed blood from his mouth and he sagged limply against the small Texan's supporting arm.

Gently laying Crouch on his back, Dusty rose and looked around. While the crowd had withdrawn in accordance with his demands, they watched with interest and muttered among themselves.

"What happened, Ed?" O'Day inquired, strolling up.

"Crouch and his wife have been attacked," Dusty explained, eyes on the other's smooth, hairless face. "He allows he'd know the man who did it."

"May I ask who it is?"

"*That* he didn't get around to telling me," Dusty admitted, alert for any hint of emotion. He had seen no sign of alarm at his first statement, nor did O'Day display relief over the second. "Maybe he will when he recovers. Until then, how about you coming with a few more of us to see what we can learn at his place?"

"Why me?" O'Day wanted to know.

"Why not you?" Dusty countered. "You're as good as a gang leader and you're intelligent enough to use your eyes and your head."

"After praise like that, how can I refuse?" O'Day conceded with a smile.

"Which of you gents wants to come?" Dusty asked, looking at the nearest members of the crowd.

Before any volunteers could step forward, running footsteps pounded across the sidewalk. Followed by the two panting townsmen and the waiter Emma had sent to collect them, Waco entered. They listened as Dusty told them what had happened. Then, while Connolly went to attend to the jeweler, Goldberg stared at O'Day.

The hotelkeeper was a badly frightened man who did not care to contemplate the implications of the night's happenings. Except for the combatants who had fallen during the recent struggle to determine which faction would control Hell, and Lampart's demise, death had always steered clear of the citizens. Outlaws had been killed in quarrels or while being robbed by others of their kind, but none of the townspeople had come to harm.

And now, in the course of a single evening three—probably four—of the citizens had met untimely, mysterious deaths.

While not concerned too much with who might have committed the crimes, Goldberg had no desire to become another victim. So he searched for a possible culprit. Every gang leader present was making a return visit. There did not appear to be any reason for one of the town's inhabitants suddenly to go on the rampage. All had warrants out for them and would be arrested if they left the security of the Palo Duro. There was only one stranger in their midst.

"Nothing like this ever happened before *you* came here!" Goldberg shouted, pointing his right forefinger at O'Day.

An excited rumble of comment rose from the occupants of
the room. The sound had an ominous, menacing ring to it.
By nature the citizens and visitors were suspicious-minded.
Most of the crowd, particularly the regular inhabitants, had
been thinking along the same general lines as Goldberg.
However, it had been left to the hotelkeeper to supply a
suspect.

"Just who *are* you, feller?" demanded a burly gang leader,
hand hovering over the butt of his low-tied Colt.

"My name is O'Day," the Easterner replied. "And, like
yourselves—or most of you—" his eyes flickered toward
Waco and Dusty, "I am a fugitive from justice who fled here
for safety."

"I've never heard tell of you," the gang leader declared.
"Has anybody here heard his name?"

Negative answers came from all sides. From his experi-
ences as a peace officer, Dusty could see all the symptoms of
a lynch mob. Alarmed by the murders, the customers and
employees were wide open for suggestions of who the killer
might be. Given just a hint, as they had been, they would
strike blindly. Darting a glance at Waco, the small Texan
prepared to intervene. O'Day beat him to it. Showing no sign
of concern, the man looked around the circle of threatening
people.

"None of you had heard another name either," O'Day
pointed out. "Yet you accept the man who bears it."

"Who'd that be?" Goldberg barked suspiciously, yet impressed by the man's demeanor.

"Ed Caxton," O'Day replied.

"Ed—!" the hotelkeeper yelped, then snorted. "Huh! We
all know what he did so that he had to come to Hell."

"You know what you read in a newspaper," O'Day corrected. "And what he himself told you."

"Mister," Waco drawled, moving to Dusty's side. "You're
asking to find all kinds of trouble."

"Ah! The younger of the Caxton brothers," O'Day answered. "I cast no aspersions on your mother's reputation,
but she did not throw a very good family likeness between

her sons. You are remarkably unalike in other ways too. Ed speaks like a man with education and breeding. Matt sounds like a common trail hand—"

"Keep talking," Waco interrupted, wondering when Dusty would take cards. "And I'm going to—"

"People are strange," O'Day went on, and something about him held the attention of the whole room. "They have preconceived ideas about how others should look. Take Dusty Fog, for example. Everybody assumes that he must be a veritable giant. Yet I have heard on very good authority that he is a small man, not more than five foot six in height. Yet, when trouble threatens, he seems taller than his fellows. He has companions too. One is part Comanche, his name is the Ysabel Kid. Another is a man of gigantic stature and handsome to boot, who might be taken by the unknowing for Dusty Fog himself. Suppose, for example, it was wanted to appear that Dusty Fog was in, say, San Antonio—instead of, say, here in Hell—Mark Counter could go there and pretend to be him."

"What Mr. O'Day's trying to get across to you," the small Texan drawled, "is that I'm Dusty Fog."

"He's *loco!*" Emma snapped, standing to one side of Dusty and with her right hand rested upon the butt of her Navy Colt. She had donned her working clothes, but wore the gun in a holster belted about her waist.

"Am I, Ed?" O'Day challenged. "Will you give me your word of honor that you are not who I say?"

"No," Dusty answered, in a quiet voice that still reached every pair of ears. "My name *is* Dusty Fog."

Half a second later, almost before the shock of the announcement had died away, before the exclamations of surprise, amazement, and anger commenced, the *big* Texan held a cocked Colt in each hand.

Knowing his *amigo,* Waco had expected such a line of action. So, an instant behind the appearance of Dusty's revolvers, the youngster's Army Colts cleared leather to throw down on a section of the crowd.

"Scatter-guns!" Emma yelled at her bartenders, almost as

quickly as the Texans made their draws. Then she produced and aimed her Navy Colt.

Grabbing the twin-barreled, sawed-off shotguns that lay beneath the counter readily available for use, the two drink dispensers lined them and drew back the exposed double hammers.

Long before any of the room's occupants could think of making physical resistance, the chance to do so with any hope of success had departed. Under the threat of the assorted firearms, to have tried to fetch out a weapon would have been suicidal.

"What do you want here, Fog?" demanded one of the gang leaders, as the general conversation died away.

"Do you reckon you can take us all in?" another leader went on.

"I don't aim to try," Dusty replied. "My work here is done, but I've come back to help you save your scalps."

"I'd listen if I was you," Emma advised. "Because if you don't, by this time tomorrow the whole bunch of you'll be dead."

15

MAKE YOUR MEDICINE,
WHITE MAN

"Well," said Emma Nene, turning slowly on her toes in front of Dusty Fog and Waco. "How do I look?"

"Like I'm seeing a ghost," the blond youngster declared. "Miss Emma, you handed me one hell of a scare when I first walked in."

"You didn't even look at Giselle, so I must have." Emma smiled.

There was justification for Waco's comment. The blonde wore a man's evening clothes, top hat, and opera cape. Not only that, but with her hair hidden beneath the hat, she had contrived to look almost exactly like the late mayor of Hell.

Coming on such a startling resemblance to the man he killed had been a real surprise to the youngster, but not enough to make him ignore the brunette. Giselle wore a brief, almost minute, white doeskin version of an Indian girl's dress. With a décolletage more daring than would have been permitted even in the most wide open of trail-end towns, the midriff bare, and the skirt extending just below her buttocks, it showed off her figure to its best advantage. The clothes and moccasins were the garments she wore when performing her "medicine dance" and being sawn in half to entertain the *Kweharehnuhs*.

"I can understand the clothes," Dusty remarked. "But the face has me beat."

"It's a rubber mask," Emma explained. "I doubt if a dozen people other than professional magicians know where to lay hands on them."

"Let's hope it stays that way," Waco drawled. "It surely fooled me."

"What's happening in town?" the blonde inquired, taking both Texans' attention from the uses to which such rubber masks might be put.

"All the owlhoots have pulled out," Dusty replied. "Your scouts, the Chinese, and the Mexicans you folks had from the *Kweharehnuh*'ve all gone. There's only the folks from the original wagon train left."

"At least you made sure that the owlhoots left without robbing us," Emma reminded him. "If you hadn't been here, they'd've taken everything they could tote off."

Backed by the menace of the lined guns, Dusty had been allowed to say his piece downstairs in the barroom the previous night. He had begun by pointing out that Hell's days as an outlaws' refuge were numbered. The town was no longer a carefully kept secret, for the Texas Ranger, the United States Army, and the authorities in Austin had learned of its existence. By that time, they would also be aware of its location, Dusty had warned. The soldiers who had helped fight off the kidnap attempt on Giselle would have delivered their report. Probably an expedition was already on its way. When it came, Dusty had gone on, it would be in sufficient strength to fight its way through the whole of the *Kweharehnuh* band.

That was, of course, Waco had reminded the audience, unless the Antelope Comanches had not decided to take matters into their own hands. Then Dusty had predicted that the latter contingency might become a fact. He had elaborated upon the significance of the attempt to capture Giselle, then on the unrestricted passage that had been granted to his party when it had become obvious that they were returning to Hell.

Everybody had accepted that the Indians must have had a good reason for wanting the brunette back in time for the allocation of the ammunition. They had also agreed that it might be to do with an attempt to break Lampart's "medicine" hold over the band. In that case, the braves would come prepared to deal with the white interlopers on their domain.

Such had been the power of Dusty's eloquence that he had persuaded his audience that he and the others had returned with the best of motives. The citizens had not been able to forget that the small Texan and his party had brought about much of their present predicament. However, with the fear of exposure hanging over him, Doctor Connolly had done much to keep the other inhabitants from making their annoyance more active. Once again, the outlaws had no reason to back up the townspeople. In fact, some of the visitors had seemed to find the situation amusing. With the lawbreakers disinclined to take up the issue, the citizens had lacked the courage to do so.

O'Day had improved Dusty's chances of avoiding a clash, by stating that he was not going to stay on and be massacred. That had brought similar comments from various outlaws. The general consensus of opinion among them had been that it would be safer to take one's chances against the forces of white law and order than to lock horns with the rampaging *Kweharehnuh*.

Satisfied that the danger of trouble was shelved, if not entirely finished, Dusty had suggested that they should resume their investigations into the killings of the evening. An examination of Crouch's safe, opened with the keys found in his pocket, proved that robbery had been the motive for the couple's murders. Although there had been no evidence, Dusty had assumed that the same cause had resulted in Duprez's and Rosie Wilson's deaths.

Explaining that he had exposed the small Texan merely as a means to avoid being lynched for a crime of which he was innocent, O'Day had insisted that his property be searched. On the way to do it, he had told Dusty how he had formed the correct conclusions on remembering what he had heard about the descriptions of the small Texan and of Mark Counter, and aided by the story he had read in the *Texas State Gazette.* It had been a piece of quick thinking on the Easterner's part, Dusty had admitted.

The examination of the man's belongings had apparently established his innocence. While his packs had held a number of clothes, they did not include a top hat or an opera cloak. Nor did he have the quantity of jewelry that had been taken from the Crouch family's safe. O'Day had no support for his story that he had not left the hotel room until going to the Honest Man, but his word had been accepted.

Later, Dusty had searched Giselle's room and questioned her without coming any closer to the solution. The saloon had closed early, but there had been considerable activity around town. Throughout the night, men and some women had been taking their departure. With the time approaching noon—the hour at which the allocation was due to take place —Dusty and Waco had just returned from making their rounds. Everything was ready for the meeting with the *Kweharehnuh,* but Hell had lost more than half of its population.

"The Rangers have got Sheriff Butterfield and your man Hatchet," Dusty remarked, referring to a crooked lawman they had met and the town's main contact with the outside world. "One of Butterfield's pigeons had come in with a message about it."

"Butterfield sent a warning?" Emma asked. "I'd've thought all he'd think about was saving his own neck."

"The message was for me," Dusty explained. "It said, 'Uncle Jules is here, has met sheriff and seen goods delivered by Mr. Hatchet.' "

"Who's 'Uncle Jules'?" Giselle asked as she draped a cloak about her shoulders.

"Captain Jules Murat of the Texas Rangers." Waco

grinned. "The gent who first learned about Hell and got us sent here."

"So it's all over, E- . . . Dusty?" Emma said quietly.

"Near enough," Dusty admitted. "Depending on today, that is. I've got a feeling something just might be about to go wrong."

"How?" Giselle demanded worriedly.

"I don't know, ma'am," Dusty answered.

"If there's any danger, I'm not getting into that box!" the brunette stated.

"Could be that'd be the biggest danger of all, ma'am," Waco warned. "Happen you don't, they'll say our medicine's gone back on us. Only this time, they'll not be caring about keeping you alive."

"Oh, lord!" Giselle wailed. "Why did I let you talk me into coming back, Emma Nene?"

"Because you're a money-hungry little bitch with no more morals than an alley cat," the blonde told her bluntly. "You came back to pick the locks and open the safe so that we could steal all the jewelry Crouch had gathered in his place. Only somebody beat us to it."

"And to Jean le Blanc's?" Dusty commented.

"It's possible that Jean had already got rid of it," Emma pointed out. "It wasn't anywhere in his place when we searched last night. He used to play a lot of poker and wasn't especially good at it."

When questioned privately by the blonde, Giselle had sworn that she was innocent of Duprez's murder. An even more thorough search than Dusty had been able to give her had also failed to produce the barber's loot. So, although still suspicious and determined to keep a close eye on her half sister, Emma had been compelled to accept the other's story that she had done no more than go to the barbershop, take a hot bath, and return to her room.

"Time we was headed out to see Ten Bears," Waco remarked.

"The Kid hasn't come back?" Emma asked.

"Likely he's getting all them fancy Comanche foods he's

always telling us about," Waco answered. "Raw, fresh-killed liver dipped in gall and such. Or they give their makings away easier not knowing him."

"I hope he's all right," the blonde breathed, noting the undertones of anxiety in the youngster's voice.

"Trust Lon to be that," Dusty answered. "If anything had been bad wrong, he'd've been out of there faster than a greased weasel. What now, Emma?"

"Giselle goes down there and starts doing her dance," the blonde explained. "Simmy follows. You'd best go with her, Ma- . . . Waco."

"I'll do that," the youngster promised. "Let's go, ma'am."

"How about those pictures of Ten Bears and the medicine woman?" Dusty asked, and the blonde produced them from a drawer in her dressing table. Taking them, Dusty tucked them into the front of his shirt. "They might come in useful."

"What happens to us after this, Ed?" Emma inquired, as the door closed behind Waco and Giselle.

"You go your way, like before," Dusty replied. "With your fifty thousand dollars, you've a better than fair start someplace."

"Do you know something," the blonde smiled. "I think I'd've come back, even without wanting Crouch's jewelry, just to see how things turned out. You're a real nice man, Ed Cax- . . . Dusty Fog."

"And you're a real smart, nice gal, Emma Nene," Dusty countered.

"You'll be wanting to kiss me next." The blonde smiled.

"I've never kissed a man." Dusty grinned.

"At least, this man hasn't any stubble on his face," Emma remarked, running her left forefinger over the mask. "I never liked your bristly old beard."

"Hell's fire, that's it!" Dusty snapped. "Now I know what's been eating at me. Emma, who did you and Giselle think O'Day was?"

"She said he reminded her of Mephisto," the blonde replied. Then her hand once more felt at the mask. "Oh, God! No. It couldn't be!"

"Who was he?"

"Simmy's partner. On the stage and in crimes. It was Mephisto who taught Giselle all she knows about picking locks and opening safes. Simmy and Mephisto organized and financed the wagon train that brought us here."

"Only Mephisto didn't make it," Dusty guessed.

"That stupid little bitch!" Emma snapped bitterly. "She had to get them both in love with her. There was an argument a few days before we left, in a hotel room. I wasn't there and don't know just what did happen. But either Simmy or Giselle threw vitriol into Mephisto's face. He ran out of the place, screaming in torment, and flung himself off a bridge into a river. His body was never recovered. There was a fast current running and everybody assumed he was dead." A shudder ran through her, but she mastered it with an effort. "Where's O'Day now?"

"Gone with the others, it looks like. All his gear's been taken from the hotel and his horses aren't in the livery barn. Would he know how to get hold of those masks, this Mephisto *hombre,* I mean?"

"Yes. Part of their act used to be a transformation trick. They'd go into boxes at opposite sides of the stage, change their clothes around, and put on the masks and make it look like they'd switched boxes. Do you think O'Day is Mephisto, Dusty?"

"I don't know," the small Texan admitted. "Anyways, it looks like he's gone. And we'd best get going to make our play for the *Kweharehnuh.*"

"I'll have to come out of Simmy's back door," Emma remarked as they went downstairs. "He always did it that way. I'm scared, Dusty!"

"Lady," Dusty drawled and kissed her. "So am I."

There was, Dusty admitted to himself, plenty to be scared about. Leaving Emma to go to Lampart's house, so that she could make the expected kind of appearance, he walked by the crater formed when the ammunition shack had exploded and through the town. On the open ground beyond the last of the *jacales,* the other participants of what might develop into a bloody massacre had assembled.

All the remaining citizens of Hell formed a nervous, worried group on the side nearest to the town. In front of them, the garishly painted wooden box had been set up ready to be used in the illusion. A gleaming, obviously sharp saw was laid on its top. In front of the box, Giselle gyrated and twisted her magnificent little body in a musicless, abandoned, and sensual dance that held the eyes of every white man present despite their anxieties. Yet, voluptuous as she looked, the mass of *Kweharehnuh* warriors behind the semi-circle of chiefs and the medicine woman showed no sign of being interested.

Studying the Comanches' ranks, Dusty noticed that only a small proportion of the braves were wearing war paint. There was no sign of the Kid. That most likely meant he was—

Dusty fought down the thought. If he and the people of Hell were to survive, he must keep a very clear head.

"Where's Lon?" Waco gritted irritably as Dusty joined him.

"Around, likely," Dusty replied. "I'm going to talk to Ten Bears."

"I'll do more'n talk if Lon's been . . . !" the youngster blazed.

"You'll stay put and keep your mouth shut, boy!" Dusty commanded grimly. Walking forward, he raised his right hand in a peace salute to Ten Bears. In Spanish, which he hoped would be understood by the chief, he said, "Greetings, *Paruwa Semenho.*"

"You I know," the *paria:vo* replied in the same language. "It was you who broke the medicine of the Devil Gun and who stood by *Cuchilo* when he spoke to the chiefs of the *Nemenuh* at Fort Sorrell. You are the one called Magic Hands by my people."

"I am the one," Dusty confirmed, knowing that to lie would be futile.

"Why are you here?" Ten Bears inquired.

"To keep the peace between the *Kweharehnuh* and my people."

"Those are your people?"

"They are white," Dusty pointed out, amused by the note of contempt in Ten Bear's comment as he had indicated the citizens of Hell. "The *paria:vo* of my people thinks they are such poor trophies that it would disgrace his *Kweharehnuh* brothers to count coup on them. So he has sent me, *Cuchilo,* and the young, brave one there to fetch them out of the Palo Duro."

"Where is *Cuchilo?"* asked the old man chief who had loaned the Kid his shield, looking around.

Dusty did not know whether he should be pleased and relieved or even more concerned by the question. From all appearances, the Kid had left the *Kweharehnuh's* village and was expected to be present at the allocation.

"Make your medicine, white man!" *Pohawe* screeched, having no desire to let the chiefs learn of the Kid's absence.

"I make no medicine," Dusty replied, wondering if the woman knew why his *amigo* had not returned. "I am a warrior. The one who makes it comes."

"I do not see him," the medicine woman declared, looking toward the town. "It is in my thoughts that he is dead."

"Then you have wrong thoughts," Dusty told her. "He will come." To himself, he growled silently. "Come on, Emma-gal. Show yourself."

Almost as if receiving Dusty's thought message, the cloaked, top-hatted figure made its appearance. Despite the warning of what to expect given by Waco, the citizens let out a concerted gasp at the sight. It might have been Lampart himself stalking majestically toward the box. Emma was no longer moving with her customary hip-swaying glide, but stepped out like a man.

On reaching the box, the substitute illusionist removed the saw and raised the lid. At a signal from the gloved, extended hand, Giselle moved forward. She hesitated for a moment, glancing around at the watching *Kweharehnuhs.* A slight shudder ran through her, but she allowed her "husband" to help her into the box. Resting her neck, wrists, and ankles in the holes carved to receive them, she made no protest as the lid was lowered into position.

As Lampart had been unable to speak Comanche or Spanish, his man, Orville Hatchet, had acted as interpreter. Dusty assumed Hatchet's role, addressing the *Kweharehnuhs* in the latter language. Reminding the visitors of how effective the white man's "medicine" had proved to be, he said that the demonstration of "Lampart's" powers would commence. Those of the braves who could not understand Spanish had his words translated for them by their more fortunate companions.

"And while the white witch is in the box, she can feel no pain?" asked *Pohawe* in a carrying voice. "Even while she is being cut in half?"

"The saw cannot harm her," Dusty replied. "She is protected by the medicine that protects all the white people of this town."

"Then make this great medicine," the woman ordered. "If it is as good as you claim, no harm will come to her or the people of your town."

Watching *Pohawe,* Dusty felt a growing sense of perturbation. He felt certain that the woman had something tricky up her sleeve. For her part, the medicine woman was conscious of Dusty's scrutiny and guessed that he was alert for possible trouble.

Small good that would do the *big Tejano* ride-plenty, she mused as the illusionist picked up the saw. Soon the palefaces' medicine would be broken and the way opened for her to carry out the great scheme.

16
I HOLD YOUR SPIRIT,
POHAWE

The Ysabel Kid twisted his head around to see who had lifted the door flap of the medicine *tipi*. It was well past sunup and he had not been disturbed since *Pohawe* had followed her companions into the darkness. However, the rawhide thongs still held him securely in their clutches and he could not do anything to escape. His eyes rested upon a bent, white-haired old *Kweharehnuh* man who stepped inside and stared in a puzzled manner at him.

"What is this?" demanded the old man.

"Set me free, *naravuh*," the Kid requested, using the word that meant respect when addressed to an old-timer. "Much death comes to the *Kweharehnuh* if you don't."

Instead of replying, the newcomer lifted his eyes and gazed with fixed intensity at the opposite wall of the *tipi*.

"I am close to the Land Of the Good Hunting, Raccoon Talker, medicine woman of the *Pehnane*," the old man announced, drawing the knife from his belt's decorative sheath.

"That is why I came to this place. Speak well of me to *Ka-Dih*, for I will do as you ask."

Moving around, the man severed the Kid's bonds. While the pain caused by restored circulation beat at him, the Texan satisfied some of his curiosity.

"Where are the men of the village, *naravuh?*"

"They have ridden to the white men's wooden *tipis*. Only the old ones, women, and children are left."

"Did *Pohawe* go with the men?"

"This is the day when she breaks the palefaces' medicine," the old man replied. "It is my thought that evil will come if she does, *Cuchilo.*"

"I am honored to think as you do, *naravuh,*" the Kid replied. "Now I must ride to my friends."

"Let me saddle your horse," requested the old man. "It is outside and I think I will never handle such a fine animal again."

"You have my thanks," the Kid said with quiet sincerity. Five minutes later, wearing his hat and in possession of his full armament, he crossed to the *tipi*'s door. Before he left, he faced the interior and went on, "And my thanks to you, Raccoon Talker."

Tired and showing signs of the great strain to which she had been subjected, Raccoon Talker emerged from her secret medicine *tipi* high on the slopes of Mount Scott. She found Long Walker waiting.

"*Cuchilo* is free," she announced. "I can help him no more this day."

"Count coup for me, *Cuchilo!*" called the old man as the Kid galloped away. "This day I die."

By riding in the direction from which he had heard the sounds of celebration the previous night, the Kid soon located the *Kweharehnuhs'* village. From there, he knew that he could easily find his way to Hell. Even if he had not been sure, the massed tracks of the warriors' horses would have served as an excellent guide. Circling the village beyond its occupants' range of vision, he urged the blue roan between his legs to a better speed.

Pausing only to slake his thirst from a stream he had to ford, the Kid traveled as a *Pehnane tehnap* on an urgent mission. He did not follow along the line of tracks, but kept off to one side of them. That was a precaution taken in case the party should have scouts watching their rear. It paid off in another way as he approached the trees that surrounded the great basin that held Hell. Four riders had quit the main body, heading at a tangent toward the wooded land.

Dismounting at the fringe of the tree line, the Kid slid free his Winchester and tucked its medicine boot under the bed-roll. Swiftly he catered to the lathered, leg-weary horse. With that done, he glanced at the midday sun as it approached its zenith. The preliminaries to the allocation of the ammunition would have commenced. If anything was going to happen, it would be during that part of the ceremony.

Darting through the trees on foot, his rifle held ready for use, the Kid moved in as near silence as he could manage. How well he succeeded showed in that his presence was un-detected by the four war ponies that stood grazing under a large old flowering dogwood tree. One of the horses had a long rifle's medicine boot draped across its blanket-covered saddle. The last time the Kid had seen that boot, it had been covering a Sharps owned by—

In that moment, the Kid saw through *Pohawe*'s plan to break Lampart's medicine. Springing to his mind, the name of the limping *tehnap* had furnished the Indian-dark Texan with the vital clue.

Kills From Far Off!

Because of his infirmity, the brave must have developed exceptional ability in using a rifle, especially at long ranges. The powerful Sharps rifle, even a model handling paper car-tridges and with percussion cap priming, was a weapon noted for its extreme accuracy. A bullet fired by it would carry from the trees to the town, retaining sufficient energy on its arrival to pass through the walls of any building—or to bur-row into the occupant of the box used for the medicine illu-sion.

Keeping downwind and taking ever greater care with his

movements, the Kid continued his advance. He did not expect that he would have to go far. With the prospect of coups to be counted and loot to be gathered, no Comanche *tehnap* worthy of the name would put too much distance between himself and his mount. Once Kills From Far Off had carried out his assignment, the quartet would waste no time in boarding their horses and heading to the center of the action.

Sure enough, the Kid had barely covered thirty yards before he found the four braves. And not a moment too soon by all appearances. Already, Kills From Far Off was cradling the Sharps at his shoulder, with its barrel supported by a forked stick that he had thrust into the ground. Holding their Winchester carbines, the other three braves stood watching with rapt attention. There was no way in which the Kid could move closer without being instantly detected. Nor could he bring himself to open fire without giving the quartet a chance to defend themselves.

"Namae'enuh!" the Kid called, snapping the Winchester's butt plate against his right collarbone.

The word brought an instant response. Spinning around, the three *tehnaps* with the repeaters gave startled exclamations and raised the weapons. On the point of pulling the Sharps' trigger, Kills From Far Off jumped slightly. In doing so, he tilted the barrel out of line at the moment of the detonation.

Flame belched from the Kid's Winchester and One Arrow died with a bullet in his head. Spinning around, he dropped his "yellowboy" carbine close to Kills From Far Off and tumbled lifeless in the other direction.

Right hand moving like a blur, so that an almost continuous flow of empty cartridge cases spun through the ejection slot, the Kid demonstrated how to attain the three-shots-in-two-seconds rate of fire promised by Mr. Oliver Fisher Winchester's advertisements. He moved the barrel in a horizontal arc as he fired, throwing the shots like the spreading spokes of a wheel.

Small Post Oak was torn from his feet by the impacts of three bullets in rapid succession, before he could raise and use his rifle. Although the third brave got off a shot, he missed. He was not granted an opportunity to correct his aim. The invisible fan of flying lead encompassed him. Four of the deadly, speeding missiles found their marks in his head and chest. He died as he would have wished: facing a name warrior and with a weapon in his hands.

Throwing aside his empty Sharps, Kills From Far Off made a twisting, rolling dive that carried him to One Arrow's discarded carbine. Snatching it up as he landed facing the Kid, he fired. As if jerked by an invisible hand, the black Stetson spun from the Texan's head. Inclining the rifle downward, the Kid responded. Struck in the forehead, Kills From Far Off made the journey to the Land Of Good Hunting.

Ceasing his operation of the Winchester's mechanism, the Kid ran by the four dead *tehnaps*. This was not the time for him to count coup in honor of the *tsukup*[1] who had set him free. That ancient warrior would not expect such an act to be committed against another *Nemenuh*. Striding through the trees, the Kid came into sight of the town. Everybody was turning his way. So far there had been no hostile response to the sound of the shooting. He wondered how long the condition of peace—or surprise—would continue to hold the two parties in check.

Everything seemed to be going satisfactorily, Dusty had been telling himself when the shooting had started. Even knowing that some trickery was involved, it had been a fascinating experience watching the saw biting through the side of the box and, apparently, cutting into the little brunette's body. He still had no idea how it was done, for the women had refused to explain. Certainly the Comanches had been suitably impressed. *Pohawe* had moved in as close as she dared, staring with great interest and clearly trying to decide how the trick was done.

Suddenly the shots had rung out: the deep boom of a Sharps, followed by the rapid crackle of Winchesters. Coming from the tree line on the rim, the lead screamed by un-

1. *Tsukup:* another name for an old man.

pleasantly close to the illusionist's top hat. Although nobody took much notice at that moment, the sound brought a very masculine exclamation of surprise in its wake.

"What the . . . ?" Waco demanded, moving to Dusty's side. Then he stared to where the shot had come from. "Look! It's Lon!"

Every eye had already been directed in that direction. Much to the two Texans' relief, their *amigo* made his appearance and loped swiftly toward them.

"It's a trick!" *Pohawe* screamed, speaking Spanish in the hope of provoking a hostile gesture by one of the white men.

"Not on our part, Ten Bears!" Dusty countered. "If there is treachery, you can blame it on your medicine woman."

"Keep your weapons down!" the *paria:vo* ordered his braves. "We will hear what *Cuchilo* has to tell us."

"I tell you their medicine is bad!" *Pohawe* screeched, but this time she spoke in Comanche.

With that, the medicine woman snatched a double-action Starr Navy Model revolver from under her peplum. Three times she fired, driving the bullets into the box's side level with Giselle's shoulders. The brunette screamed and started to struggle convulsively.

"She can be hurt in the box!" *Pohawe* shrieked. "I told you—"

As surprised as everybody else by the medicine woman's actions, Dusty Fog responded fast. Even in his haste, he used his head and did not act blindly. He remembered that the photograph of *Pohawe* had been in the outer position when he had placed them inside his shirt. So he extracted the correct picture and left that of Ten Bears concealed. Gripping the top corners between his thumbs and forefingers, he held it so that the woman could identify it.

"I hold your spirit, *Pohawe!*" Dusty warned. "If you—"

"I fear no white man's medicine!" the woman interrupted, turning her revolver in Dusty's direction.

Instantly, the small Texan ripped the photograph down the middle. Even as the fragments fluttered from his hands,

Pohawe's body jerked violently. The top of her skull seemed to burst open and she crumpled lifeless to the ground.

On the slope, the Kid had read the implications behind Dusty's and *Pohawe*'s actions. Knowing that his *amigo* would hesitate before shooting a woman—even one as evil as her—the Kid had removed the need for him to do so. Skidding to a halt and whipping up his rifle, he had driven a bullet through the back of the medicine woman's head. By doing so, he had demonstrated in a satisfactory manner that some aspects of a white man's "medicine" could be deadly effective.

Half a dozen braves, those most deeply involved in *Pohawe*'s scheme for the reconquest of Comancheria, bounded from the crowd. The woman had planned badly, for her faction had been gathered in one place instead of scattered among the other braves. It proved to have been a costly error.

Two died almost immediately, their rifles still not at shoulder level, for Dusty did not hesitate to defend himself against armed, desperate men. Showing the devastating speed and ambidextrous control of his weapons for which he was famous, he drew and fired the twin Colts simultaneously. Those of the *Kweharehnuh* who had not seen him confront the two Unionist fanatics and their Agar Coffee Mill "devil" gun learned how he had gained the name Magic Hands.

Slightly less rapidly, Waco tumbled the third and fourth of the braves from their feet. The fifth fell to the last bullet held by the Kid's Winchester. Screaming out his war cry, the sixth leaped to wreak his vengeance upon the white "medicine man."

With a heave, the illusionist overturned the box and dropped behind it. Its lid burst open as it struck the ground, allowing Giselle's bloody, lifeless body to roll out. In the dive for cover, the cloaked figure lost its top hat. Although the attacking brave sent a bullet into the box, he missed his intended target. While he was still working the repeater's lever, four Colts and Ten Bears' rifle spat at him. Any one of their bullets would have been fatal.

"I'll kill any brave who raises a weapon against the white people!" Ten Bears announced.

There was no need for the *paria:vo*'s warning. Obviously *Pohawe*'s medicine had gone very bad, so those who had considered following her lead now changed their minds. Not another weapon was lifted and the warriors stood impassively awaiting the next developments.

"My thanks, *Paruwa Semenho*," Dusty said, holstering his guns on becoming satisfied that there would be no further need for them where the *Kweharehnuhs* were concerned. "I regret having to kill your men."

"They would have killed you," Ten Bears pointed out. "And the white medicine man."

"Are you all right, Em- . . . ?" Dusty began, turning toward the overturned box. "What the . . . Where's Emma, O'Day?"

The figure that had risen still had the face of Simeon Lampart, but it was not topped by feminine blond hair. Instead, the skull was completely bald. For the first time Dusty and Waco realized that the illusionist was taller than Emma, and noticed the deep-set, glowing eyes.

"In Simmy's house," the man answered in O'Day's voice.

"If she's dead—!" Dusty growled.

"She's not," O'Day interrupted. "She'll have a sore head, but nothing more. I'm like you, I respect and admire Emma. So I contented myself with clubbing her insensible. I had to do it. She would never have willingly let me step in as her understudy."

"My apologies, Ten Bears," Dusty said in Spanish, turning his eyes toward the *paria:vo*. "I must talk to this man."

"We will wait until you are finished," Ten Bears promised.

"Why'd you do it, O'Day?" Dusty inquired, giving his attention to the man once more.

"So that I could become the next medicine man of Hell," the illusionist replied. "It struck me as a most lucrative proposition."

"It might be," Dusty admitted, "if the town wasn't closing down."

"Why should it close down?" O'Day demanded. "The ammunition is waiting to be handed over—"

"Only the medicine's been spoiled," Dusty replied, indicating the box and the motionless woman on the ground beyond it. "The town's done, *hombre*."

"Perhaps not," O'Day purred. "I think that I might yet save the situation."

"Not while Dusty and me can stop you," Waco growled.

"I know it wouldn't be any use offering you shares in the concern," the man declared, left hand rising as if to rub at his forehead. "So I must make certain that you cannot interfere with my arrangements."

While he was speaking, O'Day extended his open, upturned right palm and rested its elbow against his side. It was an innocent-seeming movement and had met with success when used against the three outlaws in Baylor County. Yet he realized that he now faced a vastly different proposition. The two Texans were not slow-witted yokels, but intelligent and lightning-fast gunfighters. Even with the surprise element of the Deringer in its sleeve-holdout rig, he would be unlikely to drop them both quickly enough to save his life.

He did, however, have an ace in the hole. Something that had saved his life on at least two occasions: once during his quest for Simeon Lampart's whereabouts[2] and last night while confronted by Rosie Wilson. Once Dusty Fog and Waco saw what lay under the mask, they would be frozen into immobility long enough to give him his chance.

"Just how do you figure on doing it, *hombre?*" Waco inquired, eyeing the wide shirt cuff above the extended, empty hand.

"Like this!" O'Day spat, and tugged downward with his left hand.

Doing so peeled off the mask and left his features exposed. There was no face as such, only a cratered, seamed, hideous mass of dirty gray flesh without a real nose or much in the way of lips. As the mask was removed, O'Day pressed

2. Told in: *To Arms! To Arms In Dixie.*

his right elbow against his ribs and set the Remington Double Deringer free. It was propelled forward toward the palm that was waiting to close upon its bird's-head grip.

O'Day was only partially successful in his assumption of the Texans' reactions to the sight of his face. What he had not known was that Dusty Fog was aware of the vitriol attack and could guess at something of the horror that must lie behind the mask.

Like Dusty, the blond youngster had suspected that O'Day carried a hideout pistol up his sleeve and was ready to counter its threat. The sight of the man's ruined features prevented Waco from responding with his usual speed. Letting out a gasp of horror, the blonde kept his hands motionless.

Fortunately for Waco, Dusty was not so badly affected. On learning about the incident that had ruined O'Day's face, the small Texan had reached an accurate estimation of how Rosie Wilson had been killed. From his memory of the sequence in which the shots had been fired and after examining the rear of the barbershop, Dusty had concluded that the woman had surprised her killer as he was leaving. Obviously she had been holding her revolver and the bull's-eye lantern. According to Emma, Rosie had known how to handle the gun. So something must have diverted her, giving the person she had confronted time to shoot. Seen in the lantern's light, that hideously marked face would have had such an effect.

So Dusty had been prepared. Yet he knew that Waco might not be so ready. Throwing himself sideways, Dusty sent his hands toward their respective weapons. He charged into Waco, knocking the youngster staggering. Even as he moved, the Remington appeared and barked. Something like a red-hot iron gouged across his right shoulder, but he knew that he had been lucky. If he had remained motionless, he would have caught the .41 ball in the torso. Pain halted his right hand, but the left completed its draw. Crashing, once, the Colt from the off-side holster sent its bullet into O'Day's left breast. The man reeled, spun around, and landed face-down on the ground.

Dusty lowered his smoking Colt and let out a long, low sigh. The assignment was over. All he now had to do was get the remaining citizens of Hell out of Palo Duro alive.

17

LET THEM LEAVE IN PEACE

Mortally wounded, Mephisto O'Day lay on top of the box, which had been set up again, and allowed Doctor Connolly to do what little he could to treat the wound. Having had his shoulder bandaged, Dusty Fog stood with the Ysabel Kid and Waco in front of the *Kweharehnuh* chiefs.

"What now, Magic Hands?" Ten Bears asked, and pointed to Giselle's body. "The medicine is broken . . ."

"I only said that the saw couldn't hurt her," the small Texan pointed out. *"Pohawe* shot her."

"The witch-woman has told you many times that the white man's medicine was a trick," the Kid went on. "Yet she could not understand how it was done. So she killed the woman in anger and paid the price. She had no medicine power, or if she had, it left her for her badness."

"Cuchilo speaks with a straight tongue," declared the old man chief who had loaned him the shield. "All along I said that she was no true medicine woman."

"This I give to you, *Paruwa Semenho,*" Dusty said, and drew the photograph from his shirt.

Watching, the Kid gave a silent whoop of delight and approval. Trust old Dusty to do just the right thing. Returning the photograph, without being asked or using it as a bargaining point, had been a masterly stroke.

"My thanks to you, Magic Hands," the *paria:vo* replied, and his deep sense of gratitude showed plainly. "What now?"

"You will be given your ammunition," Dusty answered. "The people have it. In return, I say let them leave in peace."

"They wish to leave?" Ten Bears inquired.

"Maybe they don't, but they will. You have the word of Magic Hands on that. Let them go and have your bravehearts give the sun-oath that they will not harm them as long as they leave the Palo Duro."

"The *paria:vo* of the Texans is right," Ten Bears admitted, throwing a disgusted glare at the bunch of citizens huddled in the background. "They would be coups only for *tuineps* just becoming *tuivitsi.* It will be done, Magic Hands."

"Captain Fog," Connolly said. "This man wants to speak to you."

"I'll come right now," Dusty promised, having translated the request and received Ten Bears' permission to finish the conversation. "Make the allocation, you folks."

"Then we can stay here?" Youseman asked.

"Nope," Dusty replied. "But you're getting out alive with anything you can tote with you."

"But—!" the undertaker began.

"Can we leave in safety?" Goldberg interrupted.

"No *Kweharehnuh*'ll harm you, I'll have their word on that," Dusty assured the citizens. "They'll let you out of the Palo Duro. So start handing out that ammunition."

Leaving Waco and the Kid to attend to the allocation, Dusty walked over to the box. Holding her head, Emma came up with the men Dusty had dispatched to make sure that she was all right. Ordering everybody else to keep away,

Dusty stood with the blonde alongside the hideously disfigured man.

"Have you ever seen a death scene in a drama, Captain Fog?" O'Day asked. "If not, you are now. I am going to play my death scene, using breath some might say would be better employed in confessing my sins."

"Don't talk, Mephisto . . ." Emma began.

"Talk is all I have left, my pet," the man answered. "So let me have my grand dying scene. I am sorry for striking you down—"

"That's all right," the blonde replied. "I've always taken lumps from one man or another."

"You're not the delicate flower you would have us believe, Emma," O'Day chided. "But it is a good role and you can play it well. You'll find the jewelry from Crouch's safe, with that which Giselle stole from Duprez, in the left-hand drawer of Simmy's desk."

"*You* killed Duprez?" Dusty put in. "I didn't suspect you of doing it."

"Why not?" O'Day inquired. "Did I impress you to such an extent with my glowing honesty?"

"Nope. I just couldn't see Duprez showing you where the jewelry was hidden. I figured that it'd take a pretty woman to get that. On top of which, I *knew* that Emma and Giselle had come back to lay hands on the jewelry."

"You thought that *I'd* sent Giselle to do it?" Emma demanded angrily.

"Nope," Dusty replied. "I reckoned that was her idea. You'd've been planning to get it without fuss and killing."

"That's what I planned," the blonde confirmed. "I kept warning her that you'd only stand by your word as long as nobody got hurt. Only she had to do it her own way."

"Come now, no further recriminations," O'Day put in weakly. "This is *my* death scene and I should hold the stage, not the supporting players."

"Go to it," Dusty requested, unable to hold down his admiration for the dying man. "There's nothing anybody can do to save you."

"I don't think I wanted saving," O'Day countered. "With a face like mine, there is nothing to live for except revenge. And even that is no longer with me."

"Simmy and Giselle were always afraid that you hadn't drowned," Emma remarked. "They knew that you'd be looking for them if you hadn't."

"And they were right. After Simmy had thrown the vitriol into my face, I dashed from the hotel and flung myself into the river. I almost drowned, but the water saved at least some of my face. Don't ask me how I got out of the river. Luck, maybe. I was always a strong swimmer. Or determination not to die until I had been avenged on Simmy and Giselle. So I lived—if you could call it living—but by the time I had recovered sufficiently, they were gone. I headed for Mexico, only to discover that they had not reached the original destination. So I wondered if something had gone wrong. I returned to the United States and began to haunt the theaters. If Simmy needed money, that is where he would turn. I had all my props, wigs, masks, everything. Few people ever saw my real face and none who did lived. Yet there was no word of Simmy. Until at last I picked up a hint about Hell. It was enough to set me to trying to find it."

"You got here in the end," Dusty drawled.

"And found that I had arrived too late," O'Day pointed out. "I could hardly believe the luck that threw me in with Giselle and Emma. It gave me a chance to see how well my disguise would stand up to old friends' scrutiny."

"It worked real good," Emma praised. "But Giselle thought she recognized your voice."

"And put it down to the workings of her conscience, I'll bet." The man grinned. "What a blow to be told that Simmy was dead. I had planned a different end for him. However, I decided to have my vengeance upon Giselle. And then I saw what a good proposition the town was. It would be a sop for my loss if I could take it over and run it in Simmy's place. First, of course, I would have to eliminate you and your companions, Captain Fog. No. Don't interrupt. I was seeking ways of doing it, when I followed Giselle to the bathhouse. I broke into the living quarters and hid in the bedroom. I saw her entice Duprez into producing le Blanc's loot. Then she killed him and carried it off with her. I wasted some time commiserating with her victim and was confronted by the Wilson woman as I left. I don't think she liked my face."

"It would have worked again, except that Emma had told me about you," Dusty commented. "So I was expecting something like it when you pulled the mask off."

"So *that's* how I failed. No matter now. Slipping away from the barbershop, I decided to make some trouble for your party. I went to the jewelers and was opening his safe when his wife came in. I killed her to silence her, then I'm damned if her husband didn't arrive. I knifed him, but he managed to run away. So I changed wigs and left the long one with the jewelry, my cloak, and top hat hidden behind the hotel's back house, then came to the saloon. It was my intention to incriminate Giselle, knowing that you would protect her and, given good luck, be killed. Instead, I found myself accused and in danger of being lynched. So I exposed your identities to divert attention from myself. May I say that you handled the situation in a masterly and efficient manner?"

"Thank you 'most to death," Dusty answered dryly. "Why did you come back to town? I thought that you'd figured the *Kweharehnuh*'d settle your score with Giselle and'd lit out."

"That's what I wanted you to think," O'Day admitted. "My real intention by that time was to become the ruler of Hell. I left my horses and property in the woods, returned before daylight, and concealed myself in Simmy's house. That was how I came to find le Blanc's loot. I knew that Giselle was too smart to have kept it on her person."

"How did you know that I'd come and give you a chance to take over from me?" Emma wanted to know.

"Ah. That, I admit, was fortunate rather than planned. I had learned how the allocation was always made and knew that, apart from myself, only you in Hell knew how to handle the trick. I had come prepared, in the hope that an opportunity might arise. It did and I took my chance."

"And near on bust my head!" the blonde stated indignantly.

"Pure necessity, my dear Emma," O'Day apologized. "I assure you that I struck as gently as I could. It was my hope to perform the trick, then amaze the Indians by a transformation to my real self. Then I would have persuaded them to kill you and your men, Captain Fog. What I didn't count on was that somebody would have plans of their own. What caused the shooting?"

"*Pohawe*, the witch-woman, was fixing to bust your medicine by having Giselle shot from the rim," Dusty explained. "Only Lon happened along and cut in."

"A woman again." O'Day sighed. "All my troubles have stemmed from women. Poor, treacherous, vicious little Giselle. I might have forgiven her for the betrayal if it had left me dead. But not for this . . ." He indicated his face. "Oh, well, it's all over now. Maybe I'll meet her and Simmy in the other hell."

Looking around, Dusty found that the ammunition had been handed out. He heard the words of the sun-oath rumbling out as the braves agreed that they would allow the citizens to leave unharmed and unhindered.

"Sun, father, hear my words. Earth, mother, hear my words. Do not let me live for another season if I do not keep this promise."

The small Texan nodded in silent satisfaction. No warrior would go against the sacred sun-oath. The people could leave in safety. The town of Hell would no longer offer its citizens a refuge, but they would escape with their lives and such of their property as they could take with them. When he left this time, Dusty Fog would have no conscience troubles to worry him.